A REVOLVER TO CARRY AT NIGHT

ALSO BY MONIKA ZGUSTOVA

Goya's Glass
Fresh Mint with Lemon
The Silent Woman
Dressed for a Dance in the Snow

A
REVOLVER
TO
CARRY
AT
NIGHT

MONIKA ZGUSTOVA

TRANSLATED FROM THE SPANISH
BY JULIE JONES

OTHER PRESS | *New York*

Originally published in Spanish as *Un revólver para salir de noche* in 2019 by Galaxia Gutenberg, Barcelona.

Excerpts on pp. 9, 13–14, 18, and 38 from *Letters to Véra*, by Vladimir Nabokov, edited and translated by Olga Voronina and Brian Boyd. Copyright © 2014 by The Estate of Vladimir Nabokov. First Vintage International Edition, New York, 2017.

Production editor: Yvonne E. Cárdenas
Text designer: Patrice Sheridan
This book was set in Minion Pro and Copperplate by Alpha Design and Composition of Pittsfield, NH

1 3 5 7 9 10 8 6 4 2

Library of Congress Cataloging-in-Publication Data
Names: Zgustová, Monika, author. | Jones, Julie, 1943- translator.
Title: A revolver to carry at night / Monika Zgustova ; translated from the Spanish by Julie Jones.
Other titles: Revólver para salir de noche. English
Description: New York : Other Press, 2024. | "Originally published in Spanish as Un revólver para salir de noche in 2019 by Galaxia Gutenberg, Barcelona"—Title page verso.
Identifiers: LCCN 2023033928 (print) | LCCN 2023033929 (ebook) | ISBN 9781635423808 (paperback ; acid-free paper) | ISBN 9781635423815 (ebook)
Subjects: LCSH: Nabokova, Vera—Fiction. | Nabokov, Vladimir Vladimirovich, 1899-1977—Marriage—Fiction. | LCGFT: Biographical fiction. | Novels.
Classification: LCC PQ6726.G87 R4813 2024 (print) | LCC PQ6726.G87 (ebook) | DDC 863/.7—dc23/eng/20230721
LC record available at https://lccn.loc.gov/2023033928
LC ebook record available at https://lccn.loc.gov/2023033929

CONTENTS

I

THE YELLOW BUTTERFLY

VLADIMIR

Montreux, 1977

1

He looked through the window at the lake, silver in the light of a timid spring sun, while he thought about the novel he was writing: *The Original of Laura*. He recognized that whenever he conferred a touching detail from his own life on one of his characters, it was quickly absorbed by the fictional world in which it had been unceremoniously dropped. Even if it did stay with him, the warmth and charm it had enjoyed in his memory began to dissipate, until after a while it became more intimately related to the novel than to his own experience.

He glanced at his son, who had just entered the room, and decided not to draw on his dearest memories for the new book. This time he would keep them to himself. He did not want his memories to end up the way the silent films from his long-distant childhood and youth had. He would not allow his work to steal the best part of his life, the part he kept for himself.

His son, Dmitri, forty-three years old now, was wearing a dark formal suit and a white shirt adorned with a splendid, pastel green tie. Tall and slim, he was like a poplar in the glory of spring. It was five thirty in the afternoon. A breeze that was very warm for March entered the open window of the little apartment in the Montreux Palace Hotel.

Véra praised their son, "You look very smart."

And it was true that Dmitri, an opera singer at La Scala in Milan, shared his father's aristocratic carriage. From his mother, he had inherited the translucent eyes and the classic features of the Mediterranean Jew.

"Are you going out this evening, Mitia?" his father asked. "You didn't say anything about it this afternoon on our walk."

Dmitri explained that a friend of his was singing in *The Barber of Seville*, which was being debuted that night at the Grand Théâtre in Geneva. The friend had left him a free ticket at the box office.

Véra wanted to know if he would eat supper with them after the opera.

He would eat something with his friends, he answered, heading toward the door. On the way, he opened a drawer in the table to pick up the key to his car, a blue Ferrari he had gotten only a few months ago, in late 1976. Véra trembled every time he went out in his car, but once again she hid her feelings. She knew very well that he had inherited his taste for cars and high speed from her.

She said only, "Where's your coat, Mitia? You need something warmer. It's just March. There will be a wind from the mountains and the lake."

But Dmitri was longing for the warm weather of spring. As he saw it, going out with no overcoat was a way to entice the heat, and so he went off into the night wearing only his elegant suit.

The next day, as he did every morning, the waiter served them breakfast at the table in one of their rooms, the one they used as a dining room, office, and sitting room in the apartment they had kept for fifteen years on the highest floor of the hotel. Dmitri blew his nose, coughed, and said his throat was sore. Véra longed to give him a motherly reproach—"See, that's because you didn't listen to me"—but she restrained herself. She only asked if it had been cold last night. Dmitri sipped a little tea and said that, when they left the opera and made their way to the restaurant, the weather had changed, and an icy wind had blown in from the Alps.

"I must have caught a cold. After breakfast, I'll lie down again for a while."

The cold turned into flu. Dmitri asked his father, who was near eighty, to please stay away from his bedroom. But he could not keep his mother out even though she was nearly as old. She took care of him all that day. The next day, she got sick. The flu had wreaked havoc that year, and the weather had certainly changed: After a hint of spring, the winter wind came back with a vengeance.

As he did every morning, Nabokov woke up at seven after a night that brought little rest. He tended to sleep from eleven until two without a break, thanks to a sleeping pill. When it stopped working, he took another and slept from four until seven. In the interim, he read. In the morning, he stayed in bed for a while, planning what he was going to write and do during the day. At eight he shaved, ate breakfast, and chatted with Véra. After that he took a bath. Clean and fed, he started writing. When the maids invaded the apartment with their brooms and vacuum, he and Véra took a walk along the lake's edge. At one o'clock, Madame Furrier, who looked like a cheerful fox, served them lunch.

She prepared it in a room where they had installed a little kitchen. Nabokov went back to writing before two so he could finish at five thirty. Then he went out to walk a bit and to buy the newspapers. He had the feeling that in Switzerland he was forgetting his English, so he read the Anglo-Saxon—especially the North American—press: *The New York Times*, *The New York Review of Books*, *Newsweek*, and *Time*, as well as *The Times Literary Supplement*. The Nabokovs had moved from the United States to Switzerland after the enormous success of *Lolita* made it possible for them to lead a comfortable life, free of financial worries. Every day Vladimir bought his newspapers and magazines at three different kiosks to spread around his business. He would joke with the newsagents, as he did with the people who worked at the hotel.

The journalists, who often turned up uninvited at the Montreux Palace, in hopes of an interview, complained that he was so conceited he did not want to see them. The staff at the hotel, on the other hand, adored him and defended him fiercely. The journalists did not understand. In their eyes, he was reserved, cold, and unpleasant. If Dmitri was in the hotel for a visit, he would explain that his father's apparent arrogance and coldness were a way to protect himself from the constant pressure of photographers and journalists who besieged the hotel. Accuracy was a virtue Nabokov valued; he thought long and hard about a question in order to give the best answer he could. For that reason, he only responded to written interviews.

In the morning, Véra got up to eat breakfast with Vladimir. She pulled her thick white hair—the only embellishment she wore—behind her ears so that it would not fall around her face while she was eating. When she had finished, she sat on the armchair in her husband's room. He got up with the idea of kissing her.

"No, Volodia, you'll catch my flu!" She shooed him away.

So Vladimir sat down again at his desk, not without some difficulty, and pretended to write, but he couldn't concentrate. He was thinking about Véra and himself when they were just over twenty...

2

...the date and the place were engraved on his memory even though fifty-four years had passed since then. It was in Berlin in 1923 on the eighth of May. Vladimir, who at that time was twenty-four years old, went to a costume ball held by the Russian emigrants. Although he didn't expect much of it, he decided to go so he could see Svetlana again, perhaps for the last time. The wound of their recent separation was still painful. He told himself that at the dance he could evade the strict prohibition imposed by her parents, who did not look favorably on the courtship of a poor writer. They insisted that she break off all relations with him. He cast his eyes over the assembly, looking for her. A couple of times he danced with one girl or another, none of interest to him. He smoked a cigarette with a few people he knew, but Svetlana was not to be seen.

He was getting ready to leave in a foul mood when he spotted a young woman in a black dress and a Venetian wolf mask that covered her forehead and nose. They danced together, smoked, and drank Rhine wine. The girl never removed her mask. It shaded her eyes so that he could only glimpse their sparkle from time to time. They were grayish blue and contrasted with the dark colors of the mask. Vladimir reminded her that she was still wearing the mask so that she wouldn't go to work the next day with that ugly snout. The young woman's lips smiled, but she still didn't show her face. Vladimir imagined then that the mysterious girl was very beautiful and that, tired of men's admiration, she was taking advantage of the masked ball to prove that she could captivate a man's attention with her intelligence and wit alone. Of course, she was also counting on her elegant figure, the shiny blond hair that brushed her shoulders, and her finely drawn lips. All this convinced him that she was sensitive.

Together they went out into the spring night, stopping next to a canal. The young woman recited from memory some verses that he had composed. At first, Nabokov laughed to himself at the solemnity with which she spoke: Her performance struck him as studied and theatrical as if she were imitating one of the hysterical characters from an opera by Verdi or she were a provincial schoolteacher giving a bombastic rendition of patriotic verses to celebrate a national holiday. But then he saw the flowering chestnuts that shone deep in the night and felt the moment was magical, almost otherworldly.

The feeling had grown with the recital and, although the nameless woman still wore her mask, she seemed closer to him. That same night, Vladimir wrote a poem about the experience.

In mid-May, he went to a country house in Provence for the cherry harvest; the cherries would be followed by apricots in June and peaches in July. Although he had not forgotten Svetlana, after hesitating for a few days, he began to write letters to Véra Slonim, the young woman with the wolf mask. "I won't hide it," he wrote,

> I'm so unused to being—well, understood, perhaps—
> so unused to it, that in the first minutes of our meeting I thought: this is a joke, a masquerade trick....But
> then....And there are things that are hard to talk
> about—you'll rub off their marvellous pollen at the
> touch of a word....
>
> Yes, I need you, my fairy-tale. Because you are the
> only person I can talk with about the shade of a cloud,
> about the song of a thought—and about how, when I
> went out to work today and looked a tall sunflower in
> the face, it smiled at me with all of its seeds.

When he went back to Berlin, a bone-dry city at that time of year, Véra had gone on vacation. Vladimir kept on dreaming about Svetlana, but when he heard that his friend from the dance was back, he looked her up. It turned out that, before the revolution, both of them had lived in the same neighborhood in St. Petersburg, that they had known many of the same people, and that, in their exile in Berlin, they frequented the same circles. In fact, they had had many opportunities to meet each other; the surprising thing was that it had only just happened. They went out for a walk in Wannsee, the neighborhood beside the lake. It was a beautiful, breezy day with a hint of autumn sadness, and Véra spoke of the times they could have met each other in the past but had not.

"Do you know what I think about those times?"

"What, Volodia?"

"Once there was a man who lost his telescope in the vast blue of the sea," he explained, as they turned a corner that gave them a view of the lake. "Twenty-two years later on the very same day—a Friday—the man ate a big fish and…he did not find the telescope in its guts. That's what I think of chance."

He had just made up the story, and it made him laugh out loud, but it left Véra cold. She still made an effort to give him her characteristic, enigmatic, very becoming half smile, a smile with the left corner of her mouth drawn up and the right, down. Seeing that his story had not found favor, Vladimir decided to amuse his companion with the kind of practical matters she always found interesting. He told her that he had just moved from the Martin-Luther Strasse boardinghouse to the Andersen. The owner of the Andersen was a Spanish woman who had spent a long time in Chile, a good cook and a cheerful woman, who was tolerant and calm. She wasn't bothered if a young writer turned up for breakfast at eleven, whether the cause was a night of work or of parties. Vladimir was delighted to find an ally in the owner and no longer to feel that he was violating the omnipresent order and discipline of the Germans as had so often happened to him in the past.

He remembered that Véra had laughed as though she were his accomplice. With that laugh she had completely won him over.

After this triumph, he found the nerve to show her a sheet of paper that he had been carrying in the pocket of his overcoat for weeks: He had prepared a list for his friend of the women with whom he had had lasting relationships before meeting her. These lists were a Russian custom that young men had learned from Eugene Onegin, the protagonist of Pushkin's novel of the same name. There were the names of twenty-eight women on Vladimir's list. That day, when the brilliance of the afternoon was reflected in the clean crystal water of the Wannsee, Véra only glanced at the paper and then put it away in her purse. After hesitating for a minute, she gave Vladimir a coquettish look. It was coquettish, but he saw it as also full of gratitude for his openness and good intentions.

Almost a year had gone by from their first meeting, and the following spring had arrived. The twenty-fifth of April 1925, Vladimir ate supper with the Slonims. In the middle of the conversation, very casually, Véra announced, "Before I forget: We got married this afternoon."

Her father laughed heartily, and his new wife, Aniuta, twenty-five years younger and Véra's cousin, did too.

Answering her family's questions, Véra explained that the wedding had taken place in the Berlin city hall and, that, following the letter of the law, two witnesses had been been present.

"Casual friends, really," she clarified.

———

Vladimir had lived in Berlin, Prague, Paris, as well as New York and other North American cities; now, whether he wanted to or not, he lived in Montreux. And he thought that, although the czars had never managed to win people over to the government's cause, the Bolsheviks had done so in record time as soon as the great contingent of intellectuals had disappeared into exile or was liquidated in other ways. After the revolution, the exiles dedicated themselves to their interests with such total impunity that they sometimes wondered if they enjoyed unconditional intellectual freedom because they were working in a complete vacuum. The truth is that among the exiles there were enough good readers to guarantee the publication of books and newspapers in European capitals like Paris, Berlin, and Prague on a relatively large scale, but because none of these writings could circulate freely in the Soviet Union, their literary activities felt insubstantial, almost illusory.

Vladimir laughed when he thought how easy it would have been for an independent observer to ridicule that almost disembodied throng, who in foreign cities imitated a dead civilization: the remote, almost legendary, even Sumerian mirages of St. Petersburg and Moscow from the years 1900 to 1916 (which, even back then, in the twenties and thirties, still seemed to come from some time before Christ). But at least, like most Russian writers from the first stirrings of their literature, these too were rebels. They were faithful to this sense of rebellion, and they had as great a sense of justice and freedom as their predecessors under the czars.

Vladimir and Véra spent the second half of the twenties together in Berlin, even though Vladimir wanted to move somewhere else. He struggled with what he saw as the rigidity and pomposity of German culture. He wrote about his feelings toward Germany in "Cloud, Castle, Lake," which he considered one of his best stories, in part because under the surface, as though it were at the bottom of a lake, it hid a completely different story, a story that, he was confident, no one would ever see.

A year after their marriage, when Véra had gone to a spa in the Black Forest with her mother, he wrote to tell her that one of his wishes was...

...to leave Berlin, and Germany, to move to Southern Europe with you. The thought of yet another winter here fills me with horror. German speech makes me feel sick—you can't live only on the reflections of streetlamps in the asphalt—apart from these reflections, and blooming chestnuts, and angelic little dogs guiding local blind men, there's also all the vulgarity, the coarse tiresomeness of Berlin, the aftertaste of rotten sausage, and the smug ugliness. You understand all this as well as I do. I'd prefer the remotest province in any other country to Berlin.

St. Petersburg, his lost city, was constantly on his mind. A little after he got married, he wrote a poem about his memories as an exile. Now he only remembered its first stanza:

O recollection, piercing beam,
Transfigure my exile, transfix me, recollection,
'midst windswept heavenly expanses,
of unfrequented back-road fences,
of street lamps with expressions...
O'er my Neva, there come to mind
those twilights like the rustling
of obliquely shading pencils.

3

He had sat down at his desk but could not concentrate on the novel he'd started. He thought of the day when slowly, as if on tiptoe, his first poem had come to him. That summer in 1914, he—a thin boy—had taken shelter from a rainstorm in the gazebo of a garden on the outskirts of St. Petersburg. The deluge was violent but short-lived. At the end, a rainbow appeared. Touched by the beauty of the scene, the boy gave voice to his first verses.

That was a long time ago. Now, seated at his desk, he arranged the blank index cards on which he planned to write the rest of the new novel, but his mind wandered.

Véra and Dmitri were sick, but he felt fine, light as he had in the past. For a year, he had been writing *The Original of Laura*. During his nights of insomnia, he saw the novel in its tiniest details, and every afternoon he filled out index cards. He hoped to have the first draft ready by the summer. He would take it with him when he went to Cannes for his holiday. Every summer they went to the Alps in search of new butterflies and to celebrate the ones they had already seen many times. They were very familiar with the region, those beautiful mountains and wonderful spots with famous, melodious names: Zermatt, Crans-Montana, St. Moritz, Davos, Evian, Verbier, and Chamonix. They had even bought a piece of land to build themselves a refuge on the heights of Les Diablerets, but they had never gotten around to having the work done and finally admitted the project was a castle in the air, even though they still owned the property.

Vladimir did not believe in time, nor in the passage of time. The greatest pleasure he took from the absence of time came when, in a landscape chosen at random, he discovered exquisite butterflies and the plants that fed them. That was the luck, the ecstasy behind which he found something hard to describe: a vacuum filled very quickly with everything he loved. It was then that he had the sensation of becoming part of the sun and the rocks and felt a shudder of gratitude toward the brilliant counterpoint of human destiny or toward the spirits that satisfied all the caprices of a lucky mortal being.

In summer it would be a year since his fall. He had been climbing a mountain and had almost reached its peak when he saw a yellow *Gonepteryx rhamni* that was bigger than usual. He raised his arm with the butterfly net to trap it, but he slipped off the narrow path. He fell and was hanging off the side. He felt both astonished and embarrassed, but he got up. The butterfly net, however, had gotten caught in some bushes. When he leaned over to reach it, he fell again. The ground pitched down toward the valley, and he could not stand up. Although he felt dizzy, it made him laugh: This fall, he thought, could make someone die laughing, like the pratfalls in a silent film. He saw that the operator of the cable car passing just overhead was looking at him. Vladimir kept on laughing, but when he realized there was no one to help him, he took fright. They would not come with a stretcher for at least three hours. Since the operator had seen an older man lying down laughing, he would have thought nothing serious had happened. It would only be on the way back down that he would realize something must be wrong and call for help. As he remembered it, Vladimir could not help but laugh again. He did it even though he understood that, due to the fall, something in his own mechanism had broken, like a clock that has become unreliable. From then on, he had been sickly and had spent whole weeks in the hospital.

So that summer he wanted to go to the sea instead of the mountains, but not just anywhere; he was longing to return to Cannes. He was determined to go there with Véra, to the place where, in 1937, they had spent months with three-year-old Mitia exactly forty years ago that summer. That was when he had had to decide between Véra and Irina, Irina Guadanini-Kokoshkin, with whom he had just spent a wonderful spring in Paris. Oh God, it was all so long ago... If he could return to the place where he had been faced with that terrible decision, a decision that, from a distance, might even be seen as a luxury. At that time, he was tall, slim, young. He was still a smoker—he lost his youthful glow when he gave up smoking, which he did in America for reasons of health—and he was loved by two amazing women. Amazing not exactly because they were great beauties; neither one was. But because they were mysterious, exceptional, quick-witted. Irina was feminine, irresistible... He could not decide between the two of them and was unwilling to give up either one.

He loved them both, each one in a different way. Was Irina really so special? Wasn't she just an ordinary girl, who felt superior to other people and to her life as a dog groomer because she wrote mediocre poems inspired by Anna Akhmatova? Was he a magician who shaped reality as he pleased? Who, like Quixote, had created his Dulcinea out of a common, if very seductive, Irina, just as his character Pnin had done with the vulgar and mercenary Liza? No matter where the truth lay, their relationship was much more than a mere affair. What happened between them marked him for life. He would swear to it, because—and here he started laughing again—Irina, unlike Véra, was interested in reading the Finnish-French dictionary.

Through the window he could see snowflakes whirling in the wind. He thought again that every time he provided one of his characters with a detail from his own life, it took root in the novel and died to him. The dear image of Irina had begun to fade when he bestowed her appearance and some of her attributes on Pnin's beloved. Irina, re-created as the beautiful Liza Bogolepov, acquired so much autonomy that she became Pnin's destiny. In Vladimir's psyche, the man began to rebel against the novelist.

He remembered that forty years ago someone in Paris had sent Véra, who was in Berlin at the time, a letter to let her know what was happening between Irina and him. Véra believed the story, and she wrote to ask him about it; he could still see her elegant handwriting. He answered,

> The same rumours have reached me—and I didn't doubt that they would slither over to Berlin, too. The slippery mugs of those who spread them ought to be smashed! I heard another version, from the old man: that I'm having an affair with Berberova. I am indeed at the Kokoshkins' rather often—and both of them are very pleasant—I emphasize "both."

Both of them, mother and daughter, as if there were no difference between them, that's the way he put it, cleverly adding Nina Berberova so that suspicion would not fall on the daughter alone. After that, he described in detail how the groups of Russian emigrants kept an eye on him. They followed his comings and goings so carefully that not a single detail escaped them, but they also got so carried away that they even made up stories. His letter was so convincing that Véra believed him.

Vladimir was well aware of his weakness for women. It was part of his very being. He was drawn to muses and had absolutely no interest in women writers. It was true that he had read Virginia Woolf, with the aim of knowing something about feminine literature, but he did not think much of her work. In fact, he had scandalized literary circles all over the world by saying that *Orlando* was an exquisite example of vulgarity. He preferred Katherine Mansfield, but, as he saw it, her fear of being banal was itself banal, and the colors she described were sickly sweet. He had not read Nina Berberova, but he found her lovely as a woman, even though she was gap-toothed. But...what eyes! And he also remembered that a week ago, in Montreux, he had invited the Russian poet Bella Akhmadulina to have supper with him in the restaurant of his hotel. She had come for a visit while she was on a tour of Europe. Vladimir was not bored. Bella was lively and likable and also beautiful...and like everyone who came from the Soviet Union, she hid her resentment and bitterness, her fatigue and pain, behind a radiant smile.

He looked through the window. The wind was herding the clouds over Lac Léman in Lausanne in the direction of Valais.

"You can't take me out for a walk today," he told Véra. "So I'll go out on my own to get a little air."

"Wouldn't it be better if...? Be careful, Volodia. It's starting to snow," she said without much conviction, knowing that her recommendations would fall on deaf ears.

"Do you know what? Do you know where we'll go this summer?"

"To the mountains. Maybe to France? To the foothills of Mont Blanc?"

"Right. We'll go to France, but not to the Alps. Instead, we'll go to Cannes."

"To Cannes? Then we won't go to the mountains?"

"There are hills and mountains in Cannes. I want to go to the sea. Don't you?"

Was she thinking the same thing he was? It was in Cannes that exactly forty years ago Irina Guadanini had come to find him.

He already had his overcoat and gloves on. He put on his cap, shouted goodbye to Dmitri, and headed out.

4

He leaned on his cane as he walked along the lake shore toward the castle of Chillon. He had to hold on to his cap with his left hand so the wind wouldn't carry it away. The rocky peaks of the Dents du Midi, still covered in snow, rose on his left. On his right, on Lac Léman, the wind whipped up furious waves that would have done justice to the Atlantic. The trees were still bare although the odd sprout could be seen. In a month, everything would be submerged in a cloud of green.

Just a few days ago, in another March snowstorm, Dmitri had ventured out as though it were July, with no overcoat, no cap ... and now he was in bed with a fever. Just like when he was little. How old? Six, yes, six years old. He,

Vladimir, was forty-one at the time, and the three of them had been forced to flee Europe. That too was in spring.

———

"Mitia is sick," Véra announced the minute Vladimir opened the door of their apartment on 59 rue Boileau in Paris.

Before setting off for America, he had wanted to say goodbye to a fellow exile, the distinguished Russian politician Alexander Kerensky, who had been at home with a number of his writer friends: Ivan Bunin and Dmitri Merezhkovsky and his wife, the poet Zinaida Gippius. When they heard that that very night—May 20, 1940—the Nabokovs would take a train to Brittany, where the next day they would board the *Champlain*, which would take them to New York, the mustachioed Merezhkovsky looked to the sky and exclaimed, "Leave Paris! And go so far away! That's crazy. I wouldn't do it!"

Zinaida, who wore heavy makeup, repeated with great affectation, like a nun in full lament, "But why are you leaving? Why, for God's sake? Why?"

Vladimir listened to those theatrical lamentations with a mixture of amusement and irritation and remembered an incident from his adolescence. At sixteen, he had paid to publish a little book, just a few pages long, with his first tentative poems. The booklet somehow reached the hands of his teacher, the redheaded, second-class poet Vladimir Gippius. The hard-hearted pedagogue laughed callously at his poems in front of the whole class. Volodia was dying of embarrassment. He would have much preferred physical punishment than being subjected to that humiliation. To top it off, the teacher handed over the booklet with its awkward poems to his cousin, the respected poet Zinaida Gippius, who read them and then told Vladimir's father to please tell his son he would never be a writer.

It was the same Zinaida Gippius who was moaning at that moment: "You're going to America? But, why? Why?"

Kerensky knew that at the end of the previous year, Nabokov had tried to raise five hundred and sixty dollars. If they wound up leaving, it meant that, thanks to the well-heeled Russian Jewish exiles he knew, he had gotten together not just the five hundred and sixty dollars, which must have seemed enormous in his eyes, but also passports for the whole family and visas for the United States. Kerensky asked about it, and Vladimir answered that they had decided to leave Paris because the Nazis were occupying country after country, and he had to take his Jewish wife and his half-Jewish son to a place safe. The Hebrew Immigrant Aid Society, HIAS, had sent a boat to pick up the Jewish refugees. The director of the organization, Yakov Frumkin, was an old friend of Vladimir's father and had wanted to thank him for the help his father had provided for the Russian Jews at the time of the pogrom, so he had provided Vladimir with a cabin at half price.

Vladimir added that he was leaving most of his notes and manuscripts and almost all of his huge collection of butterflies in the basement of his good friend Ilya Fondaminsky and that he was taking only what was most important: two thousand pages he had prepared for a course on Russian literature that he hoped would provide him with a living and a means of keeping his family in America, a few other notes and manuscripts, and his most precious butterflies.

While he was looking at the paintings on the wall, Bunin suggested they would do better to take a bus to Le Havre and not a train.

Vladimir was smoking one cigarette after another. "That was the original plan," he explained. The boat was going to set off from the port of Le Havre, but the German army was advancing so fast that Cherbourg had been chosen instead; however, that too had been changed. Finally, the port of Saint-Nazaire in Brittany was decided on. "We have to board there tomorrow and take off as soon as possible."

"Don't go to Brittany by train; take the bus. I've heard that all the French trains will be dedicated to the transportation of matériel," Merezhkovsky said, insisting that he take Bunin's advice with his customary pomposity, as if everything Bunin said were worth its weight in gold.

Vladimir said his goodbyes and took the Métro home. He would leave the keys to the apartment with the doorman, and he and his wife and son would set off for the train station, in hopes that it was still open.

When he got home Véra told him that six-year-old Mitia had the flu and that his fever had gone up to 104 degrees, which meant that his condition was dangerous.

They would have to go to the station no matter what. As they had already sent a trunk on to the port with their belongings, Vladimir's notes for his courses, and a small selection of his most prized butterflies, they had little luggage. They returned the keys to the doorman and headed out to the station in a taxi, stopping by a Russian doctor's house on the way.

"His fever is rising. I definitely do not recommend that you travel," Dr. Kogan-Bernstein told them, with a shake of her head.

"We have no choice. We don't have any other option," Vladimir answered.

"Change your tickets for another boat. Personally, I insist that the child needs to rest."

"It's the last boat we can travel on," Vladimir repeated.

The doctor wrote a prescription for the child while she still showed her disapproval.

They bought first-class train tickets for a private compartment with bunks so that Mitia could be as quiet as possible, and they gave him a sulfa drug every four hours. He slept all night, although early on the fever made him so restless that he threw off his covers again and again, had hallucinations, and screamed in his sleep. Véra did not get a minute's rest. She kept covering him up and holding his hand. Vladimir went out into the passageway repeatedly to smoke by the open window. At midnight, when he went in to take over, he whispered in Véra's ear so he would not wake up the boy.

"I'm afraid that tomorrow they won't let us on the boat."

"Why not?" Véra was shocked.

"If they notice his symptoms, they may be afraid he will spread an unknown infection."

Véra shrugged her shoulders. The only thing that worried her now was the danger her son was in.

When they woke the boy up at seven the next morning to give him another dose of medicine and dress him, he smiled at them as if he had returned to life. His eyes were bright and happy, and he was excited about the boat and the trip. His fever had broken.

They made their way from the train station to the port while the child, who had regained his hold on life, skipped along, holding both parents' hands.

They had one less worry.

Three weeks after the Nabokovs sailed to New York on the *Champlain*, the Germans bombarded Paris, and the building on rue Boileau where they had lived was totally destroyed. In a search of Ilya Fondaminsky's apartment, the Nazis threw out all the manuscripts they found, including those that Nabokov had hidden in the coal cellar, and they destroyed his huge collection of butterflies. After the raid, Fondaminsky's granddaughter recovered the loose pages and the butterfly wings that were scattered all over the street, and in 1950 Nabokov received them in America. But the Nazis sent Ilya Fondaminsky to a concentration camp, where he died, like Sergey, Vladimir's brother.

5

Vladimir continued his walk along Lac Léman under the trees whose bare branches whistled in the wind, but those memories had distressed him. He thought about Dmitri, his Mitia, in bed in the hotel with the same high fever he had had almost forty years ago. His son had not even told him goodbye. He was probably sleeping, poor thing, or perhaps hadn't even had the energy to respond.

Vladimir turned to go back so quickly that his cap fell off. He bent over to pick it up, but a gust of wind got there first, carrying it away. He kept going, and when he was about to bend down for it again, the wind carried it off a few more steps. Finally, a young man showed up, grabbed it, and handed it over to him. Vladimir felt ashamed when he thanked him. How embarrassing! Luckily no one else had seen his efforts to retrieve the cap. Old age is humiliating. Not in itself but because it puts a man in awkward situations.

He was happy that, when they got to Montreux twenty-five years ago, they had taken rooms in a hotel instead of renting an apartment as they had originally planned. In the hotel, they would always have help, the staff would even pick up their prescriptions at a pharmacy for a little tip, and they would not have to worry about cleaning or shopping, the everyday nuisances of ordinary life. It was already clear that they would live in Montreux. Véra had chosen the place to be close to Mitia, who worked in Milan, and it was also close to her sister Elena, who lived in Geneva.

"Montreux is very cosmopolitan," she insisted, "it's between the lake and the Alps, and your editors can get there by car or train without any problems."

Vladimir was not convinced. He would have preferred to live anywhere in the States, although, if he had a choice, he would have opted for California or Arizona, but Véra was totally opposed to the idea, and he knew that once her mind was made up, there was nothing to be done.

In front of the hotel elevator a small crowd had formed, and while he waited, he got nervous, overcome again by his strange fear for Mitia. He went up to the sixth floor, the highest one, and headed directly to Mitia's door.

Véra met him, dressed in her bathrobe. She was as white as a sheet.

"How is Mitia?" he blurted out.

"The doctor came. He has a bad case of the flu, and in the afternoon his fever rose to over one hundred and one. The doctor prescribed acetaminophen. The girl on room service brought us a tablet with his tea, and Mitia took it. He's sleeping now, and he told me to tell you to stay away from his room."

"Prohibitions are meant to be ignored. Has he eaten?"

"He's not hungry."

"We'll have to insist. And...how are you?"

"I'm not really sick. It's just a cold with a touch of fever, but don't get close to me."

"Go to bed, Véra. I'm going to make tea for the three of us. It'll be good for me too."

"I'll take care of it."

Nabokov insisted that his wife go to bed while he prepared a big pot of tea. He took a full cup with some cookies to Véra's room. Then he put a second cup on a tray, along with a dish of cold duck left over from lunch and a few slices of bread. On another plate, he laid out some sweets filled with apricot jam from Valais, Dmitri's favorites.

He opened the door. His son was sleeping, so he left the tray on the night table that had been cleared. He felt that Mitia needed something else: a book, of course! He picked up two volumes and debated between *The Divine Comedy* and *The Iliad*. Finally, he decided on *The Divine Comedy* and left it on the night table by the tray.

Then he sat down in the armchair and watched over his sleeping son.

6

He began to think about their arrival in New York. In customs at the port, they could not find the key to the trunk, which held all their belongings. Finally, the police had had to force it open. Besides the books, manuscripts, and butterflies, there was a pair of boxing gloves, because Vladimir was teaching Mitia to box. The two policemen put on a glove each. Making a lot of noise, they pretended to fight. That was the Nabokovs' welcome to the United States: a hint of what awaited them, the writer thought and smiled.

Living in exile in Germany and France had been easy: Sometimes Vladimir had the impression he was still in

Russia, since thousands of Russian emigrants were living nearby. Taking on the United States had been a different story: Its values and culture were utterly unlike what he had known in Europe. At the start—and not just at the start—the Americans seemed to come from another planet. "None of my novels," he thought, "really described what it was like to be in exile, the constant perplexity and misunderstanding." How many times had he felt ridiculous? How many times had he gotten mad at people for not seeing what was clear to him? And the worst anguish was caused by realizing that he would have to change his literary language. Véra was always going on about it. Every time he took notes in Russian, she reminded him, "In English, please." Véra knew it by intuition; her sixth sense told her, and his friends, both writers and literary critics, ultimately confirmed the same thing. Edmund Wilson, Mary McCarthy, and the others knew what they were talking about: If he did not become an American writer, he would never amount to anything in the United States.

Véra was determined they use English. He told himself that in his case, inspiration had always been like an electric current, an impulse. He was dying to write, but to write in Russian, and suddenly Russian was forbidden. Anyone who has not had that experience cannot imagine the anguish it involves. He saw English as an illusion, a poor substitute. But there was no going back. Giving up his Russian, that was so flexible and so dear to him, and taking on a language when he was less than a hundred percent comfortable with its nuances, was one of the tragedies of his life. He was often overwhelmed by the sensation that his phrases made no sense, that he himself did not understand them. How could he expect readers to follow what he wrote! He remembered his childhood, his English nanny, the nights he spent with his parents reading Dickens or Stevenson in the original, his university studies at Cambridge, and he wondered which version of English was his. Little by little, and with the feeling that he was engaging with something beyond his grasp, of being an impostor, a fraud, he began to create his own language, an American English written by a foreigner. After many tries, a baroque English began to flow from his pen. Of course, it did not have the rhythm of his native Russian, although, even in his mother tongue, he had always written very, very slowly. He felt that the more he concentrated on style, the less likely he was to keep a hand on the plot, which dissolved in the mist behind the words and the synonyms and the antonyms and the synonyms of the antonyms, all of his word games. He loved word games, which also came naturally to Irina Guadanini. He once remarked on this in front of Véra. She grew pale, but later on she began to try it too, although her choices tended to be behind the times.

Véra had a certain quality: When she was transcribing *Lolita* and other novels, she was never taken aback by the erotic charge of many of the passages. The most she might do was comment that they were written like prose poems. The opening of *Lolita* flowed from Vladimir's pen as if it had a will of its own. Those words gave the whole novel its rhythm and melody, its atmosphere of nostalgia. He repeated them to himself: *Lolita, light of my life, fire of my loins. My sin, my soul. Lo-lee-ta: the tip of the tongue taking a trip of three steps down the palate to tap, at three, on the teeth. Lo. Lee. Ta....* The words were untranslatable. Only readers who knew English well could appreciate them; that is, only a *happy few.*

He laughed when he thought of the academic dissertations whose authors tried to decide if Nabokov was a Russian writer or an American writer. The last Soviet encyclopedia defined him as an American author. They must be right, he thought. An American author who was rotting in a second-rate Swiss town among provincials and country people. He had lost his flexible Russian years ago, and he felt that, now exiled in Switzerland, he was losing his English. But Véra was convinced that it was the ideal spot for both of them, that they could concentrate on their work there. One thing was clear: Véra was afraid that he might dream again about cosmopolitan women like Irina, about American actresses...like the divine Marilyn! What a woman! All breasts and roses...

And the revolver in Véra's purse...

He poured his suffering over language and the experience of being a foreigner into *Pnin*. Professor Timofey Pnin, a double like him, spoke a peculiar English with an odd pronunciation and an unknown accent,

> The elderly passenger sitting on the north-window side of that inexorably moving railway coach, next to an empty seat and facing two empty ones, was none other

than Professor Timofey Pnin. Ideally bald, sun-tanned and clean-shaven, he began rather impressively with that great brown dome of his, tortoise-shell glasses (masking an infantile absence of eyebrows), apish upper lip, thick neck, and strong-man torso in a tightish tweed coat, but ended, somewhat disappointingly, in a pair of spindly legs (now flanneled and crossed) and frail-looking, almost feminine feet.

Critics, professors, and students often asked who Pnin really was. A buffoon? A character so comic that even American professors imitated him? Or, on the contrary, a pathetic figure, a Pierrot, a rejected lover who became a laughing-stock? Only a few of the readers realized that Pnin was his creator's noblest and purest character. He was Nabokov's Don Quixote.

In his bedroom in Montreux, their son slept quietly, his forehead pearled with drops of sweat. Vladimir snuggled down into the armchair. During his walk, the wind had worn him out, and he felt drowsy. He remembered a dream he had had in 1943 when he had been in the United States for three years. In the dream, he saw his brother Sergey on the bunk of a Nazi concentration camp dying in excruciating pain. Waking up, he told himself it was crazy, that Sergey was safe in Austria, living in the palatial home of Hermann, his partner. But he didn't feel easy because he believed in dreams. If you pay attention, they always tell you something about yourself, about other people, about the present and the future. The next day, Vladimir received a letter from his brother Kirill, who had gotten his address through *The New Yorker*, which had published one of his stories. In the letter, Kirill wrote that Sergey had died recently in a concentration camp near Hamburg. His death was brought on by starvation and the stomach problems associated with the condition. Later he found out that in 1943 they had arrested Sergey in Berlin on a charge of homosexuality; however, five months after that he was freed from the camp thanks to the help of their cousin Onia. Since he did not want to keep on living in Berlin or anywhere else in Germany, a country he despised, he found work in an office of Russian emigrants in Prague. He never hid his disdain for Hitler's Germany and the Nazi regime, which he criticized openly. One day he got into an argument with some German intellectuals who assured him that German culture was the loftiest and the best in the world. Apparently, Sergey argued with them until daybreak, attacking their delusions of grandeur and their chauvinism. His criticism must have reached the wrong ears, and the authorities began to keep an eye on him. They arrested him again when he helped a friend escape to England: This time they accused him of spying for the British and sent him to another concentration camp.

The news distressed Vladimir. In the last few years, he and Sergey had not been close. Nabokov had been critical of Sergey's homosexual relationship and also that his partner was a German. Nonetheless, after reading Kirill's letter, he realized that he had missed something important. Sergey had been a hero. Vladimir felt proud of his brother's openness, sincerity, courage, and determination. He was ashamed of having shouted at him in front of their family and their friends. He felt even worse because there was no going back. At that moment, sitting in an armchair in the hotel in Montreux, he was inundated by a flood of cold sweat. Even though time had passed, he was still ashamed of himself.

He got up to pull the covers over his son. He went to the window to concentrate on a memory brought on by the thought of Sergey.

7

It happened in the spring of 1907 in Vyra, in one of the Nabokovs' summer houses on the outskirts of St. Petersburg. After a long, copious late lunch, the hosts and the guests all took their coffee out on the terrace. He was eight or nine at the time. His uncle Vasili Rukavishnikov, a diplomat whom everyone knew as Ruka, stopped him. Uncle Ruka was an elegant man who always wore a violet carnation in the buttonhole of his pearl-gray coat. He liked to recite poems that he had written in French.

"Let's stay in the dining room, where the sun is coming in. Is that all right with you, Volodia?"

He seated the boy on his lap, caressed him, and whispered in his ear that Vladimir was his kitten. The little boy felt embarrassed. It was a huge relief when his father came back into the dining room. His father was put out with his brother-in-law. The cold insistence of his words made that clear: "Basile, people are waiting for you. We are on the terrace." Then he sent the boy to his room. Despite this rebuke, Uncle Ruka visited Volodia that night. He asked the boy to show him his little collection of butterflies, and while they looked at it together, his silky mustache tickled Volodia's face. His caresses progressed to groping and became increasingly insistent. These meetings were both pleasant and unpleasant, tempting and repugnant at the same time. They went on for four years.

One summer Uncle Ruka went to his own country house, which bordered the Nabokovs'. Vladimir, who was twelve at the time, went to the station to meet him. He saw his uncle—a character from a Proust novel, specifically the homosexual Charlus—come out of the long international train. He was traveling with half a dozen huge trunks, and he always bribed the railroad man on the northern express to make an illegal stop at their tiny provincial station. Ruka glanced at his nephew and said, "How sallow and plain you have become, my poor boy."

One time, promising him a magic gift, he strode ahead with his short legs and white, almost high-heeled shoes; he took Vladimir to the nearest tree, delicately snapped off a leaf, and offered it to him with the following words, in French, "For my nephew, who is the most beautiful thing in the world, a green leaf." Once that was said, he did an about-face and went off.

The day Vladimir turned fifteen, Ruka took the boy to his office and, in his correct but dated French, announced that he had made the boy his sole heir: "Now you may go. *L'audience est finie.* I have nothing more to say."

It was an inheritance worth millions and millions of dollars. In the same tone, Humbert Humbert, the protagonist of Vladimir's best-known novel, had given Lolita, who was seventeen years old and married by that time, money as a wedding gift. It did her no good because the girl died in childbirth. Something similar happened to Vladimir, since, after the October Revolution, his inheritance from Uncle Ruka was worthless.

Every summer, between the waves of the Atlantic and the beaches of Biarritz, little Volodia fell in love with a different girl—from the Serbian Zina to the Parisian Colette—and he wanted to try out Uncle Vasili's games with them. His parents came on him by chance one time in an unlighted street holding a little girl's hand and sent him to bed forthwith. Another time, he went to the movies with Colette, and there they planned a romantic escape together.

Fifty years later, Vladimir described Uncle Vasili's games and his own feelings as a young victim in *Lolita*. He had to write the novel to throw light on what he had experienced in his childhood. He merged it with the pleasure he had felt at sixteen embracing Lyussya and the trauma when he lost that first love. He took up the theme of the seduction of children again in *Pale Fire*.

He was becoming more and more convinced that the memory of Uncle Vasili's games was what kept him from accepting his brother's homosexuality and, in fact, homosexuality in general. He was criticized more than once for his attitude, especially in America. He had been wrong. If only he could take it back...

Nabokov turned from the window and looked at his son. In his fever, Mitia had thrown the covers off again. Vladimir covered him up with the eiderdown, touched his hair gently to avoid waking him up, and then kissed his burning forehead.

"For God's sake, Volodia! What are you doing? Do you want to get sick?"

Véra was in the doorway, wearing a robe, majestic and arrogant as usual, reproaching him in a loud whisper. No, he didn't want to get sick, he mumbled in answer. But he had no reason to worry about getting sick, he said to himself. He felt fine and was certainly not going to get sick. Véra had no way of knowing that he had been thinking about his brother and was trying to compensate by giving his son the love he could not give Sergey now.

"Véra," he said when the two of them had gone into the sitting room. As on many other occasions, he felt that his wife would help him.

A memory came to him. After their wedding, Véra had gone with her mother to a spa in the Black Forest, and he sent her a letter. That summer he wrote in a light, playful tone about sunbathing, playing tennis, and bathing in the Wannsee rather than about what he was writing. At that point, he was working on a single narration, the apparently frivolous "A Fairytale" about a seducer of women who is both inept and insatiable. Vladimir was very taken with the story. When Véra returned from the Black Forest, she took charge, and pointed him in the direction she wanted, so that his following letters from Paris and London were written to show that he wasn't being lazy, but that he was taking his job seriously. Vladimir smiled and shook off the memory.

"Véra," he continued, thinking about his brother once again, "in a letter I sent when you were in Berlin and I was in Paris, I told you about a lunch I had had with Sergey. It was at La Bastide, near the Odéon. I remember clearly that in the Luxembourg Gardens the yellow leaves were starting to fall from the chestnut trees. Do you remember the letter?"

"It was when you were in Paris in the fall of 1932. I can find it for you right away. All of your letters are in the bottom drawer. Sergey... Sergey... Here it is."

I had lunch today near the Luxembourg Gardens with Sergey and his husband. The husband, I must admit, is very pleasant, *quiet*, absolutely not the pederast type, with an attractive face and manner. But I felt somewhat awkward, especially when one of their acquaintances, a red-lipped, curly-headed man, approached us for a minute.

Vladimir thought about the unfair and unfounded aversion to homosexuality he had felt until he found out that his brother Sergey had died in a concentration camp. But no, that repulsion was not unfounded: It was because he had suffered his Proustian uncle's abuse. Uncle Ruka had died in 1916, in the Saint Maur hospital near Paris. He was still young, still on his own, and he had had a heart attack. Sebastian Knight, the protagonist of a novel with the same name, had died in the same way.

8

Madame Furrier, with her little blond mustache like a fox's fur, had prepared supper: an array of sweet and salty crepes, with a white wine, a Chablis from Grand Cru Grenouilles. Vladimir turned on the standing lamp, which gave off a weak light, and sat down across from Véra, who had set the table, placing the text of the day next to his plate. Like every night, it was intended to prove why a meal was not a waste of time. That day, however, he did not pick up the pages. Supper smelled delicious, especially the salmon crepe.

"Do you remember when we were living in Paris, and sometimes we didn't have money for food?" she asked him in a soft voice.

Vladimir served the wine and thought it was a shame Véra only let him drink one glass over dinner. She was afraid he would lose neurons, a side effect, she believed, of drinking. Vladimir did not believe in such things, and when he could, he would serve himself another glass. He could not help laughing to himself about the time Véra invited an editor to have a drink in their apartment. She left the open bottle on the table and took the editor to Vladimir's office to show him something. When they came back into the sitting room, Vladimir saw that Véra was looking for the bottle, and he told her straight off, "I threw it out the window."

Afterward he was thoughtful: Paris was about more than hunger. After the Russian Revolution, almost all the people with creative energy and open minds abandoned the Russia of Lenin and Stalin and moved to Paris or Berlin or Prague.

"Once," Véra continued, "Nina Berberova, the one who was pretending to be a writer—you know who I mean? She also went to America although that wasn't until the war, and now she teaches at the University of Philadelphia. Well, Nina brought us a chicken. I put it on to cook right away. You were in bed."

Vladimir knew that Nina was not "pretending to be a writer" but that she was one, even though he had never read what she wrote. It was something he knew without needing to read her work. But he didn't say a thing: Véra would get mad and say he was defending Nina. He pictured her, a delicate brunette, extraordinarily attractive and elegant even in her poverty, bringing them a chicken, its lifeless eyes like little pinheads in a face that hung down, leaving a dribble of blood on the floor and on Nina's black overcoat. Vladimir laughed out loud.

"Don't laugh, Volodia. It offended me that she, who was also poor, made a point of showing us, without the least consideration, that we were poorer than she was. She took pity on us as if we were beggars."

Vladimir kept on laughing. He knew that Nina had helped them out of respect for his talent. She herself said once that Vladimir had redeemed and justified the whole postrevolutionary wave of exiles with his work. So he interrupted his wife. He felt that he had to speak up. "But we ate the chicken happily. It fed us and did us good. What's bad about that? Her intention was good."

"No, it wasn't. She did it on purpose. And afterward, she wrote a stupid article about it. That's what made me maddest."

"I had the flu, and Nina's chicken helped me recover. She really did want to help. I remember the scene very clearly: You thanked her, you smiled at her, it seemed like a friendly exchange."

"Nina did not want to help. She came to humiliate us. So, I smiled at her? That smile was a mask. It's clear that you don't know me, and you've never understood me."

Vladimir did not try to answer. This was an argument that Véra made often: "You've never made an effort to understand me." Perhaps she was right. The truth is that he had never known how to interpret that smile of hers in which the left side smiled and the right side seemed to frown in a gesture of sarcasm and bitterness. He preferred to think about other things. What Véra said had brought another memory from that time: Yosif Gessen, the editor of the newspaper *Rul* (and of his first books), generously and kindly allowed him to fill the literary supplement with his immature poems about things like the blue nights of Berlin and flowering chestnuts, but also about his nightmares, the kind that were familiar to every political exile:

On certain nights as soon as I lie down
my bed starts drifting into Russia,
and presently I'm led to a ravine,
to a ravine to be killed.

He had talked to Nina often about the anguish of the refugees. That was so long ago! But, in spite of the years, Nina emerged in his imagination as alive as if he had traveled forty years back and they found themselves together in L'Ours, the Russian bistro, and the two of them cracked up laughing. He ignored Véra's bad temper and, to distract her and himself as well, he drank a little wine and began to tell a story about Nina. As he told this anecdote, he almost forgot about Véra's presence and seemed to be speaking to himself.

"We were together in L'Ours, since we had some business to talk about: a literary prize and an article. For many years, Nina was the partner of the great Russian émigré poet Vladislav Jodasevich, a fragile, embittered man, full of irony, sarcasm, and black humor, and a good friend of mine. She showed up with her usual Oriental air, lithe, wearing a pearl-colored dress, and I . . . you'll remember that at thirty-eight I was what I am no more: dark-haired (this thin hair is the little that is left), slim, and good-looking. That day I was wearing a white shirt. We ate blinis (the ones from the cook at L'Ours were famous for being thin and crunchy and tasty) with smoked fish and pseudo caviar. We started washing them down with vodka, and later the maître d' brought us a bottle of red wine. We laughed and toasted everything. According to Nina, my Petersburg *r* vibrated without stop.

"'Where do you write, Nina Nikolaiev?' I asked her.

"'In the summer, at home on the little tippy table with a view of the chimneys of Paris or in a café. In the winter, I don't write at home. I don't have any heating. Like everybody else, no?'

"'Not like everybody else. I write primarily in the *toilette* if you can give such a fancy word to the little room in my suburban apartment.'

"'Why in the bathroom, Vladimir?'

"'Mainly because the sun shines on it all morning. And also, although it's a secondary consideration, there's no furniture in the apartment.'

"'You two live in an empty apartment?'

"'Completely empty. When Véra or my son wants to go to the bathroom, I have to interrupt my writing. But they know and are very considerate. They try not to drink much.'

"Nina laughed and laughed about this, and she toasted my peculiar writing desk.

"'There is always a chair and a table, whichever I prefer, but never the two things at once. I'm going to give you a piece of advice as a writer, Nina, even though you don't need it. Don't forget that, although it has its inconveniences, because it's a room people use, the toilet tends to be the quietest place in an apartment.'

"The maître d' came to fill our glasses. I paid and excused myself because, unfortunately, I had an appointment related to work. Nina said that with me out of the way, she could at least enjoy what was left of the food without interference. Later, Nina and other Russian émigrés who were eating there that day told me what happened afterward. Two young Russians, apparently a painter and a new novelist, approached the table where Nina was eating alone after I had gone.

"'Nina, I would like to introduce you to my friend Nikolai Vasilievich Makeyev, a painter, a disciple of Odilon Redon, a journalist, a politician, and the author of a book called *Russia* that has been published in New York,' said the writer.

"'So, he's a Renaissance man,' Nina replied with an ironic smile. The young man smiled and looked at Nina without blinking.

"'Isn't your friend Nabokov a little conceited and a show-off?'

"'No. What makes you think that?' Nina cut him off.

"'People say that when he's out in society, he pretends not to know his best friend or calls somebody Iván Ivanovich knowing very well that his name is Iván Petrovich. You'll see that one day he'll call you Nina Alexandrovna! And he also likes to change names in order to use his irony and sarcasm to show that he's superior. For example, the book *In the Hidey-Hole*, he calls *In the Asshole*.'

"'I don't know where you are trying to take this,' Nina answered dryly. 'Vladimir Vladimirovich has his oddities, but who doesn't? Did you know that when *The Defense* came out in *Sovremennye zapiski* in 1929, I read the novel twice, one time after another.'

" 'Twice?' Nikolai was surprised.

" 'Yes. I was holding a demanding work, written by a great author, a mature and complex author. I suddenly realized that out of the fire and the ashes of the Bolshevik Revolution and the Russian exile, a great author had arisen like a phoenix.'

" 'You sound serious.'

" 'Yes, I do, because I realized then that in the future our existence as exiled writers had some meaning. Nabokov's writing justified my whole generation.'

" 'I have read his articles in *The Latest News*, Nina Nikolaievna. How can you speak of a generation and of justification? Hasn't he said more than once, and with a sense of confidence that, I have to admit, exasperates the reader, hasn't he said that not just writers but everyone else is alone? Does he sound like he's thinking about his generation? Nabokov has earned his place in literature, and there's no doubt that he will hold it a long time, but does that mean that other writers, including you yourself, will only survive in his shadow?'

" 'I'll respond to your arguments one at a time. I know that every individual is a world, a universe, and also a hell in himself. Of course, Nabokov can't rescue a mediocre writer with his own immortality. But he does offer an answer to the uncertainty of all of us who live in exile, who have been disgraced and humiliated, to those of us who, often unfairly, are ignored, to all of us who have been left by the wayside.'

"And then she added in a low voice, speaking more to herself than to her companions, 'That miserable, absurd, unhappy, poor, cowardly, sad, devastated, hungry Russian emigration that I am part of! Last year the great poet Joda-sevich died. He was skeletal, laid out on a mattress with the sheets in rags, with no money to pay for a doctor or even for medicine. This year I went to see Nabokov and found him in bed, sick, in a deplorable condition. Who will be next?'"

Véra had stopped eating and was quiet, withdrawn. She remembered the jealousy she had felt at that time for the attractive, intelligent, and original Nina.

Vladimir was also pensive. He was thinking that in Paris and Berlin at the time the Russian émigrés spoke of only one thing: Russia and their fate as expatriates. He had composed a short poem on the theme that he included in *The Gift*, his novel on exile:

Thank you, my land; for your remotest
Most cruel mist my thanks are due.
By you possessed, by you unnoticed,
Unto myself I speak of you.
And in these talks between somnambules
My inmost being hardly knows
If it's my demency that rambles
Or your own melody that grows.

Véra remembered once again the chicken that she had torn from Nina Berberova's hands to put straight into the oven.

They looked at each other and laughed. Vladimir took her hand and kissed it tenderly. That night they enjoyed each sip of Chablis more than ever, for its taste and its honey color, and each bite of crepe as well. They even found one filled with caviar.

9

Madame Furrier, with her red-painted smile under that fox mustache, took the tray with the leftovers off to the kitchen. She placed two cups on the table and between them the teapot with their nighttime tisane.

Vladimir served Véra the infusion of lemon verbena, then filled his own cup and looked at the framed photo that sat on the table. Mitia had taken the little picture on the summit of La Videmanette. Of course, his father was wearing shorts and had the butterfly net in his hand. He was strong and dark-haired, and he was taking in the view of the Gstaad valley. How powerful he had felt! At that time, he was still walking for hours every day. He climbed mountains and felt a dizzy pleasure when he reached the summit. That day, at the top of La Videmanette, he told Mitia that he had done everything he had planned to do and had wanted to do in his life and that he was enormously happy.

In the meantime, Véra went off to find the corrections of his novel *Transparent Things*, now translated into French, in order to go over them again. Her husband would read the corrections after she had finished.

He remembered how often he had hesitated when he was writing that novel. He had been away from the States for five years, and the American atmosphere was almost out of his reach. Where should the novel take place, then? He finally decided to locate the story in the Swiss Alps, although the protagonist would be American and the female lead Swiss with Russian roots. But he still felt there was something false about the novel, that the action was happening in an artificial world that did not exist, as had been the case with *Ada, or Ardor*. There was no help for it. It was too late to move the action back to the United States. To avoid thinking about it, he settled himself on the sofa to catch up on the day's ration of papers in English. The headlines danced before his eyes: "KLM accepts responsibility for the collision of two planes over Tenerife, in the Canary Islands. The number of dead has reached 583." "A commando from the Baader-Meinhof gang shoots General Buback, the attorney general, and his chauffeur." "The earthquake in Bucharest leaves 1,500 victims." "The Spanish neofascist commando AAA that wants to put an end to efforts toward democratization in Spain opened fire in Atocha. Five people were killed in the massacre and four more injured."

He put the newspapers aside. His throat hurt, but he didn't mention it so as not to alarm Véra. He drank the hot tea and tried to get comfortable on the sofa.

"I'm going to lie down in bed. I didn't sleep well last night," he announced and went to his room.

The wall between the two rooms was thin so that each one was always aware of what the other was doing. As he closed the curtains, he saw that Venus was shining over the lake, Venus, the Milky Way … the sky was covered with stars. When he went to his room, Véra, who was worried, had kept an eye on him. She was upset to see him bent over, dragging his feet on the carpet. She turned to her corrections again.

In his room, Vladimir thought about Véra. She had always helped him, as she had done at Wellesley in the forties and Cornell in the early fifties. When he started at Wellesley, he had entered the full classroom with an air of decision, vigor, and happiness, like an actor going to collect an Oscar. The young women looked at him with shining eyes: He was tall and, even though he was bald and thirty years older than they, elegant, sophisticated, and different. Most important, he was a foreigner who had lived in a variety of European capitals, his classes focused on interesting and demanding material, and, more than that, he, Professor Nabokov, was the first European most of them had ever seen. Their makeup was intended for him. Vladimir was sure of one thing: Véra knew that her husband had become a myth on the campus. He felt flattered, and more than one of these young women appealed to him. Some of them flirted with him openly, and he was afraid of all this attention because he felt very tempted. He did not flirt with them but, when Véra was not around, he was very attentive.

"Ah, Miss Rogers, I see that you're wearing something new," he said when one of his favorite students came back from Easter break wearing an engagement ring.

When he entered the classroom in the winter, he shook the snow off his greatcoat, took off the big rubber boots he was wearing, in the Russian way, over his polished leather boots, and later Véra helped him with his overcoat. She hung it on a hanger and then she took off her own cap, gloves, and overcoat. No, that was wrong. Véra sat in the middle of the first row and kept her overcoat on, draped over her shoulders. In her purse, she had a little box with the chalk. She opened it and put the pieces in order according to color. During the class her husband was teaching, she either handed him the chalk or wrote notes on the blackboard as he dictated. Didn't that bother her? Vladimir wondered. How had he let her do it? Who knows, but he did.

Why was he thinking about that tonight? Véra herself had offered. She was the one who wanted to sit in the first row and listen to his brilliant lectures. Like Madame Perov in "Bachmann," a story he wrote a few years after meeting Véra. He predicted the nature of his relationship with his wife in this character. Véra was Madame Perov seated in the first row of the concert hall in front of the superb Bachmann, listening with veneration to his magnificent performance on the piano. Near the end of the story, the pianist's agent says that Bachmann never loved Madame Perov. Véra asked him in surprise if the pianist had really never loved his fairy godmother. She could not believe it, but if Vladimir had written it like that, then it was true: Bachmann did not love her. Art does not lie. In the story, he had presented a great artist and a woman whom the artist did not love. He did not love her, but he needed her desperately for his art. To love and to need: There is a great difference between the two. While he was writing the story, Vladimir thought vaguely about himself and Véra. He liked her combination of feminine charm and the very unfeminine tenacity with which, he believed, she made sure that his books got written. The same thing that Bachmann had liked in Madame Perov.

Véra was almost certainly aware of the rumors about Professor Nabokov and his student, the beautiful brunette Katherine Peebles: that in the dark winter afternoons they held hands as they walked about the campus; that they strolled around the park and through the streets, stopping to drink a cup of hot chocolate in one of the cafés on the way; that he had sometimes wrapped her up in his big quilted overcoat; that they kissed in the dark streets. Véra did not know that in this way Vladimir was repeating, as if it were a scratchy old record on an ancient gramophone that he never grew tired of hearing, his memories of Lyussya and of Svetlana and Irina Guadanini as well. Véra did not know; she must have told herself that attending her husband's classes was a lesser evil. And it was useful: Véra kept him in line. When she did not stay in the classroom, she waited during his afternoon classes, parking the car by the student union so she could get him home and away from harm as soon as possible.

It was the same at Cornell, with its coed classes. The students understood this arrangement in their own way and admired the dignity with which Véra performed this rather undignified service. That's what they thought, but Vladimir told himself that Véra was happy with the situation. Her shiny hair was pearly white, undyed, and she wore it straight down to her shoulders, framing her face. She didn't wear a hint of makeup on her clear, pink skin and for jewelry only a string of pearls that stood out against her black sweater. Her carriage was always very upright. She held her head high and always wore a half smile as if everything were perfect, as if serving the maestro, as she put it, were the most natural thing in the world.

Vladimir knew that the young men, afterward, whispered to each other that Véra was the noblest woman they had ever seen. And that she knew he was still interested in the feminine sex, whether it was girls or grown women. He himself had told her many years ago that his sexual desire had been awakened by his romance with Lyussya, his first love, a romance that had been brought to an abrupt end. In the summer house in St. Petersburg, the two young people had hidden in the depths of the garden, where people stumbled upon them from time to time. Forty years later, Professor Nabokov ventured out in the evenings to stroll in the snow with that flirt Katherine just as young Vladimir and Lyussya wandered along the wintery streets of St. Petersburg, looking for a dark corner between the canals where they could hide from the eyes of strangers. Did Véra realize that the trauma of his first love, which had ended too soon, had stayed with her husband for good?

He wanted to write the story of a man who preyed on little girls. It was a compulsion, and he turned the theme over in his mind for decades. He had written *The Enchanter*, but that wasn't it; he wasn't satisfied with that novel. He took up the theme again in what would have been named

The Kingdom by the Sea until, in the summer of 1948, he
came upon a newspaper article that related a criminal case
involving Frank La Salle, a mechanic, who had kidnapped
an eleven-year-old girl named Sally Horner and for almost
two years had her at his mercy. Keeping just ahead of the
law, he and his prisoner moved from one place to another
in the United States. Vladimir was fascinated by this terrible story, especially since he recognized echoes of his own
childhood experience in it. He had always left little winks
at the reader in his works, and in *Lolita* the protagonist
wonders at one point, "Had I perhaps done to Dolly what
Frank La Salle, a fifty-year-old mechanic, had done to Sally
Horner, who was eleven years old in 1948?" thus revealing
the source of the novel's structure. Sally wound up rebel-
ling just as Lolita would rebel, and a few years after their
rebellion and their liberation, both the real girl and the fic-
titious girl ended up dying.

Vladimir needed to write the truth about his uncle
Ruka. He had of course referred to him in *Speak, Memory*, in which he pictures that refined uncle who made the
eight- or nine-year-old Volodia sit on his lap and, while
he caressed him, murmured loving words and crooned
little songs to him in a low voice. Remembering that first
encounter with Uncle Ruka, he wrote the scene in which
Humbert Humbert reaches a climax with Lolita on his lap,
sure that the little girl will not realize what is happening.

Vladimir always needed to feed on his memories. "I
have never understood the need to invent things"—he
thought—"things that have not really happened this way

or that way. I prefer to leave the work of imagination to my heart and then leave the rest to memory, which is like a long shadow of personal truth."

He had worked on *Lolita* every afternoon until well into the night. On Sundays, he stayed in bed writing. He couldn't help it. Lolita was his alter ego as the young victim of a depraved uncle, but the novel also reflected the desperation of a writer who longs to write in his mother tongue but isn't allowed to. In the book, he listed details of the vulgarity of popular American culture. Its vulgarity scandalized him even though he recognized that in the United States he was happier than he had been as an adult in any other country, and he admired the culture of interpersonal relationships. "I have always found my best readers there," he said with a sigh.

But the real paradise, he thought, lying in his bed, had not been America. The real paradise had been his childhood. Vyra, the Nabokovs' summer house on the outskirts of St. Petersburg, with its gardens, lakes, and paths through the woods. "I can see it so clearly," he murmured to himself, "the bedroom, the wallpaper with roses against a blue background, the open window. The scene only needs the oval mirror hanging over the leather sofa on which Uncle Ruka is seated, calm now, Proustian, devouring the pages of a battered old book with great pleasure." A sensation of security, of contentment and summer warmth invaded his memory. "In comparison with such a potent reality, the present here is just a shadow. The mirror overflows with light. In the room in Vyra, a bumblebee brushes against the ceiling. Everything is as it should be. Nothing will ever change. No one will ever die."

Lyussya was a real paradise too. He saw her for the first time in the summer house at the end of 1915, at a musical gala. He was sitting a few rows behind her, and he was drawn to her thick, chestnut-colored hair pulled up with a ribbon of black velvet. After that he saw her in the little coppice of birch trees, standing quite still, except for her eyes. It was as though she had been engendered there, in the middle of the birches, the firs, and the moss, with the silent perfection of a mythological creature.

He remembered that, at the end of September, layers of fallen leaves piled up as deep as their ankles. In the little clearings, antiopa butterflies with a cream-colored border on their wings were flying about. The unpredictable tutor, who was supposed to be taking care of him and his brother, often lurked in the bushes with his old binoculars to spy on Lyussya and him, but the gardener found the spy and told the lady of his house, Volodia's mother. The boy took his beloved girl places that were the subject of his delirious dreams until, in a small pine grove, he left his fantasies behind and fulfilled his desires. Since Uncle Ruka was not in residence that summer, they were free to wander around the enormous, leafy, two-hundred-year-old park. On the side of the path that led there, Vladimir broke off dahlias and gave them to her.

When winter came, they wandered in the urban parks of St. Petersburg along tree-lined avenues covered with a lacework of white frost, and they curled up against each other on the frozen benches. They frequented museums, where they found silent, out-of-the-way rooms dedicated to mythological scenes that were of interest to no one. The Hermitage put beautiful corners at their disposition, especially one behind the sarcophagus of the Egyptian high priest Ptah.

The spring of 1916 was, in his mind, typical of St. Petersburg. With the warm weather, masses of flowers were in bloom. Lyussya with her hair cut short and a new white hat, leaning against the back of a bench in the Alexandrovsky Gardens. Next to the public restrooms, an explosion of lilacs, the tolling of the cathedral bells, the fresh air stirring the undulating surface of the Neva. And it was followed by the wonderful summer. He saw that Lyussya was happy, standing on tiptoe to reach the branches of the cherry trees so she could gather the shining fruit. The whole world and its trees were whirling in her smiling pupils and, because of her efforts, under her raised arm a dark spot of sweat was staining her yellow dress. They ventured into the depths of the forest that was lined with moss, they swam in a bay out of a daydream, and they swore eternal love next to the corollas of the flowers that she loved to weave into dainty crowns. At the end of the summer, Lyussya went back to the city and found a job.

Even though he would never have admitted it, even though he wanted to think he had broken things off with her so he could pursue other loves, it was clear that sunny little Lyussya could not bear his absurd and unjustified attacks of jealousy, and…she left. Yes, it was Lyussya who abandoned him.

He remembered then, with an intensity that rent his soul, a late afternoon in the spring of 1917. After the winter of their inconceivable separation, he had run into Lyussya on the train. They spent the couple of minutes between stations side by side in the passageway of the railcar, which was swaying and screeching. Lyussya was in good spirits, thanks to a chocolate bar she was eating piece by piece, while he was embarrassed and weighed down by his pain. On one side of the tracks, in the bluish swamps, the dark smoke of the burning peat fused with an enormous, amber-colored setting sun, which, at that time of year, would never set entirely. That same night, Aleksandr Blok wrote down a reference to the peat smoke and the sky that was in front of the two of them. Now Vladimir saw a connection between the landscape and the moment he saw Lyussya for the last time. She got down from the train and turned to look at him before disappearing in the half dark of the tiny station. The air was filled with the scents of late spring, the jasmine, and the mad racket of the crickets. Even now, so many years later, nothing could soothe the intense pain that he had felt back then.

Years after they parted, he wrote about Lyussya in his first novel, *Mary*. Here he faithfully described their relationship, starting with their initial outings on a little boat, continuing with their steamy encounters in hidden corners of the garden, and ending with the letters she wrote to him from her safe haven in Ukraine after the revolution and her final exile in Crimea.

And many years later, he took up the theme of their summer paradise in the country houses on the outskirts of St. Petersburg. In *Ada, or Ardor*, Ada, who is twelve, and Van, fourteen, chase butterflies. Together they pull apart the caterpillars, they stretch out on the pine needles and the moss, they race down avenues lined with tilting old statues in Ardis Park, their own planet, their Antiterra. The ignorant critics wrote in their reviews that the novel was about the author and his wife. What nonsense! The dim-witted imbeciles did not even see the obvious: For a relationship to be tempting it must be forbidden. Only Vladimir knew that in his world the sensual Ada and the seductive Van were transfigurations of Lyussya and himself, of Irina Guadanini too, and even, in a way, of himself and his uncle Ruka.

10

The next day, when Vladimir got up for breakfast, his voice was hoarse, and on the day after that, he could not speak at all. He realized that he had a fever, but he did not want to stay in bed. He wanted, with all his heart, to be healthy and strong. However, he did lie down more and more often, and after a few days, he couldn't get up. On March 19, he checked to see if he had fever: It was over 100 degrees. Véra called the doctor, who sent an ambulance. An hour later, he was in the Nestlé Hospital in Lausanne, with a diagnosis of the flu.

After a few days in March that were warm for the season, a long, cold, rainy spring with frequent bouts of sleet set in. Nabokov went home to the suite at the Hotel Montreux, on May 7, so he and Véra could celebrate the fifty-fourth anniversary of their first meeting at the costume party in Berlin on May 8. The thermometer on their balcony showed that it was only 41 degrees. The trees around the lake were bending with the force of a north wind from the Alps, and people tried to protect themselves, doubling over and carrying umbrellas that the gusts of wind blew inside out. Vladimir closed the orange curtains to give them a feeling of sun and warmth. The heating system in the hotel was running as if it were winter.

On May 10, Ellendea and Carl Proffer came from the University of Michigan in Ann Arbor. They were publishing Nabokov's complete works in Russian through Ardis, the university press. They brought five volumes that had already been published, and they signed a contract for the rest of his work. Nabokov was happy that his problems with publishing houses had ended. He had had them for most of his life even though Véra had been a huge help, taking care of the correspondence and financial arrangements. He was enormously pleased that a serious press was publishing his complete works in Russian, and he was even happier to be back home from the hospital. He told an endless string of jokes: He had an Andalusian daughter, he had sat on top of a hot teapot someone had left on the sofa, and so on.

On May 18, he wrote in his diary: "Am I seeing things? 99.5 degrees. Is it starting all over again?" On June 5 his fever went up to over 100 degrees. He returned right away to the hospital, where they diagnosed the cause as "unknown." Even though he was sick, he was still in a good mood, making plans to move to the Côte d'Azure with Véra as soon as possible.

"In Cannes, the swallows will fly through the streets just as they did forty years ago. Don't you remember, Véra?"

Véra did not answer.

"And in the summer the parks in Cannes are full of white butterflies, the *Pieris rapae*," he went on, immersed in his daydream. "Someone told me it means good luck if a white butterfly flies into your house."

Véra said nothing.

"Could she have realized that it was Irina Guadanini who told me about the white butterflies?" he wondered. Of course, it was possible. Knowing her, it was even likely. He quickly changed the subject to his health.

"Cannes, yes! It will be sunny and warm. I'll get well there. As soon as I'm a little better, we'll leave for the south of France," he promised.

But he didn't recuperate. Every day he seemed weaker than the day before.

"Our patient is getting better," one of the doctors told Véra a few days later when they had left the room together. He reinforced his comment with a cheerful wink.

"You have a great gift for observation. Enormous, really. You see everything, doctor," Véra responded with a frown. "On the other hand, I think we're losing him."

She left the doctor in the hall, his mouth hanging open, and went back to the room. She found her husband shuffling through the sheets of paper of his half-written book.

"Véra, if I don't have time to finish *Laura*, you must destroy it."

Véra did not answer.

"Is that clear? Destroy it, with no compassion. Promise me, my love."

Véra was thinking not about the novel but that Vladimir was confirming what she had just told the doctor. She agreed without listening to him.

"You're not listening, my love. You must destroy my manuscript. Agreed? Don't do what Max Brod did with Kafka's work."

"What do you mean?"

"Kafka begged his friend Brod to destroy all his work after he died. Brod, however, did not respect his friend's wishes. He turned over all the manuscripts to Kafka's editors, and, to top it off, he wrote a biography of Kafka that was full of lies," Vladimir explained, giving her such a naughty wink that, for a moment, Véra felt a little relieved and, calmer now, promised to do what he asked.

11

According to the calendar, it was July 2. Vladimir came back to his senses and left the world of daydreams. He felt weak. Was he really dying? He thought it would not be like this. He thought about a poem that he had written some five years ago:

> How I loved the poems of Gumilyov!
> Reread them I cannot,
> But traces have stayed in my mind,
> Such as, on this think-through:
> "...And I will not die in a summer house
> from gluttony and heat
> but with a heavenly butterfly in my net
> on the summit of some wild hill."

Was it the strange daydream that left him feeling so despondent? No, he thought. The strong pills were to blame, the perfect drugs they fed him in the hospital. He didn't know whether he wanted to submerge himself again in his dreams and finish the projection of that vision or not. He would call it "A meeting by the sea."

In an old issue of the Russian magazine *Rul*, published in Germany, that his sister Elena had brought to the hospital a few weeks ago, he saw that Irina had died the year before. The obituary did not mention the cause of death. They described her as a poet and published four of her poems, which were mediocre at best. But those sentimental verses about kindred souls who live far apart and spend their lives looking for each other were, he was sure, about him, Nabokov.

Irina Guadanini, his beautiful witch, had died on October 28, 1976. He calculated that she must have been seventy-one. He turned to his diary to find what he had written on that day, written before he knew about her death: "Today I haven't felt like doing anything. I've felt strange, and I've dropped everything I've started on."

The image of Irina on the beach affected him for hours. When Véra and Mitia came in, he didn't feel like talking. He pretended that he was too tired.

"We shouldn't tire him. He must hear us, but he doesn't have the energy to respond."

But he was still happy that they had come to see him as they had every day. If he was feeling low, one of them would spend the night in his room, on the bed they made up on the sofa.

"Open the window, Mitia."

Mitia did what his father asked and kissed him on the forehead, as usual. Then on the cheek. This was new.

"What's this about, Mitia? We've never done it before!" Vladimir joked and realized that his voice was hoarse.

Mitia didn't answer. He just smiled a little, taken aback and touched. Véra caressed her husband's hand and then his face.

Vladimir understood that they were saying goodbye to him. The happiness of having them beside him came to an end. His eyes filled with tears. Dmitri asked why he was crying.

"Because the white butterflies have gone. They are flying somewhere else, and I don't see them anymore."

A nurse entered the room, where the window was still open. As usual, she left the door open too so a little draft blew through it. The nurse sneezed once and then two more times in quick succession. Dmitri hurried to close the door. The patient's condition got worse quickly. His eyes were closed and his breathing irregular. His skin was waxy.

It was seven in the evening. The sun was still high when a yellow butterfly flew through the window and fluttered around the room, coming to rest on the bed. Dmitri, leaning over the sick man, remembered that one day his father had told him that the Greek word for butterfly is *psyche*, which also means soul, and that the ancient Greeks believed that the *psyche* flies out of the mouth of someone who is dying as if it were a butterfly.

Vladimir opened his eyes. The butterfly was reflected in both of them. He thought for a second that the last thing he would ever see would be a *Gonepteryx rhamni*, then closed his eyes again and stopped breathing.

II

IRINA ON THE BEACH

Cannes, 1937

1

As she was leaving the station, a leaf fell at her feet. The first autumn leaf, she thought, but then corrected herself: "The first autumn leaf I've noticed." The contrast between the summer sky and the fallen leaf surprised her.

The sun had still not come out even though it was a quarter of eight. Her light step and slim figure sometimes attracted the gaze of men in the street, but her face was too plain to be considered beautiful. As the sun began to shine, gilding roofs and the upper balconies, she descended through the streets that led down to the sea. She had left her case in the baggage area of the station. In her handbag, besides her sunglasses, she had her bathing suit, a small towel, and her coin purse.

She was dazed after spending a sleepless night on the train. Unable to doze off, her nerves on edge, she wasn't sure how this visit would turn out. Partway down, she sat on the terrace of a café in a street that was still half dark. It afforded her a glimpse of a sparkling green strip of the sea. She ordered a coffee and a croissant, but when she had barely tasted the food, realized that she couldn't keep anything down. She paid and headed to Place Frédéric Mistral. There she took a good look at a house where three bathing suits were hanging out to dry: a man's, a woman's, and a child's. She realized it wasn't a good idea to stare at the window of the building, so she rounded the corner and made her way to the wharf. She wandered along it for a while and then headed back slowly. When she reached the square, the window of the house opened and a woman's hand reached out for the man's bathing suit and then the child's and then disappeared into the dark inside the apartment. Irina didn't move; she stayed where she was, waiting.

A tall man with a little boy came out of the house. At thirty-eight, he was still slim and supple. Irina did not start following them until they had walked some distance. The man and the little boy walked through a park planted with palm, olive, and ficus trees. Then they entered a dark underground tunnel that led to the seafront, and they picked up their pace. Irina walked behind them feeling more and more resolved. She knew that she would overtake them. In the tunnel, which muffled the sound of footsteps, she began to run. When she was back in the daylight, she slowed down, but about a hundred meters ahead, she saw the man striding on quickly and almost dragging the boy with him. She had no choice but to pick up speed if she hoped to reach them while they were still on the promenade. She would not catch them on the beach in her high-heeled sandals. She needed to have a serious talk with him, and the beach would keep the encounter, which might be their last, from becoming too solemn. But that meant that if they turned left now and went down the stone steps to the sand, her trip would be wasted. She walked as fast as she could, no longer caring if they heard the sound of her heels on the pavement. She was closing the distance between herself and the two silhouettes. The man slowed down and, without stopping, helped the child blow his nose into a handkerchief. From walking so fast, she began to see spots before her eyes and was afraid she would fall, but her high heels kept on moving, while the sea breeze caressed her short golden hair and played with her light, translucent skirt. Her heels played their own melody on the pavement, and, almost in spite of himself, the man turned and then froze, staring at her.

"So you have come," he said, more cool than surprised, when she drew up, "in spite of my writing you."

At that moment two short old people who were carrying buns and a baguette for breakfast passed by. They turned to the man and also greeted the little boy: "What a glorious day! Good morning, little one! After supper, bring your wife to our house. The Dujardins are coming too, so we can play a game of bridge."

The man, who was still affected by his unexpected encounter with Irina, did not say a thing. He just managed to give the old couple a faint smile and nod his head.

The couple kept going, and the boy tugged on his father's hand, urging him to go to the beach.

Irina saw that another acquaintance was heading their way. He waved at the father and son. So they wouldn't get away, she murmured, "I'm here. I have to . . . we have to . . ."

The middle-aged man who had just waved to them crossed over to their side at an almost military pace. He greeted Vladimir in Russian and looked at her with curiosity. With an excessive curiosity that was almost insolent, Irina thought.

When the man went on, the little boy started tugging his father's hand again, insisting they go on, but his father ignored him. "Be still!" He looked at her as if he could hardly believe she was there. Then he hung his head.

"How long are you...?"

"Calm down. I'm leaving today. You needn't worry," she answered although she had reserved a room for three nights in the hotel across from the station and had no intention of leaving so soon.

"Papa, I'm going. I want to swim. Give me my bathing suit."

"Wait a minute, Mitia. We're going right away," he told the little boy, still looking at Irina. As indifferent as he had been before, he told her, "Wait, don't leave yet. We do need to talk."

Irina hardly recognized him. He had never spoken to her in that way.

"What hotel are you in?"

"In the one across from the station. What's its name? The Traveler's Hotel? The Foreigner's Hotel? The Englishman's Hotel?"

She was nervous, and she could not summon the name of the hotel where she had reserved a room. And she had also forgotten she'd just said that she was leaving that very day.

She had pictured it all differently. She remembered that, just a few weeks ago, he had written saying that if she wanted to, they could go away together. Go anywhere. Perhaps to another city on the Riviera where it is always spring; yes, spring was her season... but now the leaves were beginning to fall. "We will go someplace else together," Irina had written him. That's how she had reacted to his letter saying that his wife had found out they were writing each other, that the situation at home was hellish.

And now the two of them were facing each other, both unnerved.

The child kept pulling on his father's hand.

"Why did you stop writing me, Volodia? What's become of all those promises that we'd soon see a light at the end of the tunnel and that light would lead us to the sun, the air, freedom?"

"I couldn't do anything. It's not worth talking about, but at home the situation was so awful that I was terrified."

Irina coughed, because she felt as if she were drowning, but she managed to control her jealousy and her misery. She told him with the greatest indifference she could muster, "Did you never think what I was feeling? Without you there? With almost no letters?"

"Don't torture me. Tell me what I can do."

"Come with me. Right now."

"I can't close the door just like that on fourteen years of a life lived without any problems."

A life without problems. He repeated these words over and over in his letters too. Irina turned on her heel.

She had heard from a distance the jingling of a bell. A little donkey with his hooves painted red was coming along the promenade. A man with a red Phrygian hat was leading him.

"I'm off. There's no point in waiting. We'll never see each other again, and that's for the best."

"Irina, please be patient. This will all pass, and things will go back to being like they were before. Wait for me, and in winter I'll come see you."

"By yourself?"

"Well…I don't know. I can't promise. But everything will be resolved soon one way or another. You'll see."

The donkey was getting closer. His bells jingled happily, and the boy pulled his father's hand again. He made out the sign on the animal's back: "Freddie. The Queen of Ice Cream."

"Papa, I want ice cream from the donkey, he's brought it for me! For me, Papa!"

And he kicked the pavement, pulling his father in the direction of the little burro with doubled energy.

The man kept on paying no attention to him and resisting the pressure. He told her in a low voice, "I have to go."

"You have to go? Then, go!"

She turned again to leave and saw that he wanted to stop her, that he was moving as if to hold on to her. She headed off, hearing between the click-clack of her heels the voice of the man shouting behind her, "Don't leave, Irina! Everything will be all right!"

2

She headed to the beach, took off her sandals, and lay down. Even through the towel, she felt that the sand was still cold after the September night. Lying down, she heard the noise of the children playing in the water. The sun was getting hotter and hotter. She wanted to get in the water, but she didn't have the energy to change into her swimsuit. She sat up on the towel and looked around her. The beach had filled up. She spotted the man. He was sitting on a towel like she was and watching the child, who was playing in the water with a bucket and showing his father something again and again. The man's towel and hers were not far apart, but he didn't look at her a single time. It was as if she weren't there. She saw a slender woman approaching the boy. The woman said something to the child, patted him on the cheek, and spread her towel next to the man's. He smiled at her as if nothing had happened, as if she, Irina, weren't there, as if she had never existed. The woman sat in front of the man; he put cream on her back with hands that were dark from the sun, almost black. Then the woman turned over gracefully and lay facedown. Irina noticed how much she was enjoying the sun and the sand, which had warmed up.

But the sun was bothering Irina. She didn't know how to escape it. She certainly didn't feel any relationship with the Italians of Cremona. At that moment, she was, more than ever, a Kokoshkin from St. Petersburg. She put on her bathing suit in a nearby changing room, but she didn't have the nerve to go into the water. Even from there, she was sure to make out his watching eyes, which she found intolerable. Besides that, she didn't have the energy for it. She looked all around her, but the children, who were fooling around with spades and pails, with inflatable rubber floats and balls and animals, were unnerving. She lay down again so she wouldn't have to see the colors of the swimsuits and the parasols, not to mention the sparkling sea and the shining sun. She didn't want to have the sun in her eyes. She would have been happier if it had clouded over, had even started raining. Yes, things would be much better with a rainstorm.

Lying down, with her face to the sun, she could not move. She suddenly heard words in Russian: "We can meet at three in the park." It was his voice, but it still sounded cold and distant. She half opened her eyes to see his head, like a cutout against the burning, noonday sun. She couldn't see his face, which was in the shade. She remembered that there was something strange in the last letters he had written her, something that had not been there before. Like the tone she was hearing now. She sat up, shook off the sand, and looked at the sea without looking at him.

3

Vladimir was also looking at the sea. He was standing in the waves, a few meters away from her. "Right now the sea is the same color as her eyes," he told himself. The thought struck him as stupid and a little kitsch. *Poshlost*, a pretty Russian word that indicated something that was vulgar, banal, and ordinary. But no matter how ordinary the image, it didn't change the color of her eyes or of the sea. In February of that year, 1937, after he gave a reading at a Parisian bookstore, that slender woman, who must have been about thirty, came up to ask if he would sign her copy of the book. All he saw was the turquoise blue of her eyes. For a moment, it took his breath away. Now he kicked the white cap of a wave to get rid of the image he didn't want to see, but it was useless. The image returned to his mind over and over. Back then in February, the young woman's likable, youthful mother had invited them both to have tea in the café. There they realized that in St. Petersburg during the first two decades of the century they had been part of the same circle. The mother was the widow of Kokoshkin, a politician who had been killed in an attack. Vladimir felt at home; he immediately sensed a bond with these women, who had lost a husband and a father in the same way that, once his family had emigrated to Berlin, he had lost his own father to a group of fanatic Russian nationalists. Irina Kokoshkina went by Guadanini, the family name of her Italian grandfather, a violinist from Cremona. Vladimir visited the two women at home a number of times. Véra was staying with little Mitia in Berlin, where—in spite of her Jewish origin—she had a well-paid job. Vladimir wrote her a letter full of admiration for the women. After a while, however, he became irritated by the mother's constant praise of her daughter. It was as if she wanted to sell the young woman to the highest bidder; he began to leave the mother out and instead focus on Irina.

They went out to see the old movies they both adored and new releases as well, discovered cafés and bistros, bookstores, and parks. Soon they became an inseparable couple who were well known in Russian emigrant circles. Later on, when Vladimir saw that Irina ran her hand devotedly over the hollow his head had left on the pillow and collected the butts of his cigarettes from the ashtray as though they were relics, he got worried and wrote long letters to his wife, begging her to come quickly to Paris, but since Véra did not know what was happening, she wasn't in a rush to go. "We should visit your mother first. I promised her we'd go," she wrote in response. He tried other methods to get her to come: "Don't you see that in Germany the sky is clouding up over your head? You're a Jew. How can you keep on living in that nest of anti-Semites? Of little Hitlers? You need to leave before they do something bad to you." But Véra answered that the Germans where she worked thought highly of her. Again and again, she returned to the theme of his mother: "We can't do this to Elena. We need to visit her as soon as possible."

Vladimir knew that Véra was right: They had to visit his mother. But there was a problem: Irina Guadanini was in Paris. He knew that he ought to go to Berlin, pick up his family, save them from the clutches of the Nazis, and take them to Prague, to his mother's, where they would spend a month or two and then all go together somewhere else, anywhere else, as long as it was far away from Paris, where the Russian emigrants were very familiar with his weakness for Irina. But he could not make up his mind to do it and instead spent days on end with Irina. He was not even interested in writing, apart from the time he took almost every day to write Véra in an attempt to ease his uneasy conscience. In spite of himself, he still felt guilty and suffered from a rash and insomnia.

Why couldn't he live without Irina? Was she that beautiful, he wondered now as he put the rubber float on Mitia, who was splashing water all over. Instead of marvelous beauties, Vladimir had always preferred slender, lively women. Irina also was good at word games. She wrote poetry, but he knew from the few examples he had seen that her verses were mediocre attempts to reproduce Anna Akhmatova's work. Somehow that great poet had inspired a whole procession of mediocrities who venerated her writing. He also knew Irina wasn't an intellectual. In fact, she didn't have much of an education. She even made mistakes when she wrote in French. But he forgot all that when he thought of Irina's very feminine tenderness and sensuality. He had been with Véra for fourteen years, fourteen wonderful years without any dark moments, he told himself in a whisper, and he repeated the words that he had used just a moment ago when he and Irina spoke of his marriage. He had only known Irina for six months, four of which he had spent away from Paris. Irina had been his spring surprise, but how could he abandon the happiness he had known in his marriage for a relationship that had only gone on for two months? He knew it was possible. He had written often enough in his novels about a passion that overwhelms common sense and takes with it everything good and sacred in life.

A month before going to Cannes, he had convinced Véra to take Mitia to Prague to his mother's house. He was waiting in Paris for his Czech visa, but in the meantime his Nansen passport expired, and the French government refused to give him an extension, saying he would have to collect it in Berlin, which he had no intention of doing. Finally, it was all resolved, so that Elena had the chance to take walks with her Volodia and his wife and child in the spring sun of Prague, walks that took them to Troja Palace through the Malá Strana neighborhood and Stromovka Park with all its rhododendrons in bloom.

Vladimir and Véra took a few days on their own to visit Františkovy Lázně, thermal springs where they stayed at the Hotel Egerlander. The spa had a shady garden with peacocks wandering around. Vladimir treated the bad rash that first a French doctor and then a Czech doctor had both diagnosed as psoriasis, caused by the state of his nerves. Each of them asked if he had been under a lot of stress lately. The thermal waters relieved the rheumatism that Véra had suffered from all year. Spending time together, he realized he regarded her as a friend, almost a sister, and that his thoughts were constantly with Irina in Paris.

After a few days, Véra received a second anonymous letter, like the one written to her earlier in Berlin. It was written in French but with a Russian handwriting, and the sender gave several pages of details about Vladimir's relationship with Irina. Once again, Véra believed it. The letter was very credible. Of course, Vladimir denied it all vehemently, and yet again, Véra chose to believe him. But his bad conscience began to torment him and made it hard for him to pretend nothing had changed. He wrote to Irina accusing himself of the "vulgarity of this pretense. Suddenly I have a moment of clarity, and I feel evil, a monster."

Nevertheless, he begged her to keep writing because he could not get along without her letters, and he sent her the address of V. Korff, the owner of a bookstore in Prague, where he was going to give a reading, so that she could write him there.

Finally, he told his mother goodbye without realizing it would be for the last time. He went to another spa, Mariánské Lázně, where he stayed in the Ville Busch with Véra, her sister, and Mitia. It was there that he wrote his story about Germany: "Cloud, Castle, Lake." It seemed he was leaving Germany for good, and he was anxious to express the repulsion with which he viewed the German mentality, but... was that really the theme of the story? It included his fear of losing Irina. Yes, he sensed that something terrible was about to happen and that he would have to give her up for good.

But once they got to Cannes, he confessed to Véra that he and Irina were still corresponding. Véra made a terrible scene and forced him to tell her the whole truth. She told him again and again that if he could not live without Irina he should go to her in Paris.

"Not now," he said miserably.

"'Not now?' How about tomorrow? Would tomorrow be good?" she shouted desperately.

Or maybe it was different. Véra did not shout, and she did not feel desperate at all. Perhaps only at the beginning of the scene. When she spoke, she was cold and dismissive. She addressed him as if he were trash. She didn't care if they separated; probably that's what he wanted.

"Not now," he repeated, consternated.

"If not now, when?"

"Not now," he repeated once more, like a monk reciting his litany.

It was stupid, but he could not avoid it. The only thing he knew at that time was that he was not going to separate from Mitia and Véra. She threatened to go off with their son so he would never see Mitia again. That would be horrible, unthinkable, but Vladimir was not sure he could repress his desire for Irina. He did not want to lose Mitia or Véra either, but he didn't have the strength to give up his lover. In those days, in Prague, he sent Irina letters full of love and jealousy.

I am always so anxious to talk to you. I don't have much time, but I can't stop writing you even if it's just a few words. I am more and more aware that I can't share you with anyone, but would you give everything up for me? I'm overcome by panic and desperation. I love you so much....

She responded with verses from the poet Julie de Lespinasse:

Je vous écris et je déchire mes lettres.
Je relies les vôtres—elles me paressent toujours trop courtes.

Vladimir could not help noticing a couple of mistakes that she had committed when she copied these French verses. But what would bother him in other people just made Irina seem closer. It made her seem human and even more desirable.

For a few months now he had been full of doubt and close to madness. He had just endured forty-eight hours of hell with his family. In spite of his desperate situation, he felt a little relieved: Everything was out in the open now.

Yes, he felt relieved, but only somewhat. He still didn't know what he would wind up doing, and he was hoping that he would not have to give up Irina. At the end of those forty-eight hours, during which neither he nor Véra really slept or ate until they were almost prostrate with exhaustion, Véra announced: "I'll give you a month to think it over. If you decide to go, please do it quickly. But if you are still living with us, your family, at the end of that time, I will understand it as a promise that you are going to stay. After that, you won't have the right to leave."

4

The atmosphere in the trattoria by the rock was pleasantly cool, but a little before three, when Irina emerged into the summer heat of the street, she felt depleted. Luckily the park was close by. She sat on a bench near the entrance in the shade of a plane tree. A leaf fell on her lap; it was shaped like a butterfly. She didn't shake it off. The park was deserted except for an older woman who was nodding off at the entrance to the restrooms in the shade of a fig tree.

The bells of a nearby church rang out the three o'clock hour. With Vladimir everything seemed urgent. When he left Prague and came back to Paris, in early June, his family had stayed in the house of one of Véra's cousins, and he with some friends, the Fondaminskys. They had four days to get together before he took his family to Cannes, where he planned to stay until the winter. Vladimir told her that, when he bought the train tickets in Mariánské Lázně, the agents had suggested that if they traveled through Germany, the tickets would be half price and they would be given tickets for the world's fair in Paris as well. They accepted, reached the Gare de l'Est without any incidents, and visited the fair that same day. There were two huge pavilions next to each other: one German, the other Soviet. The family didn't like that. So much vulgarity and absurdity, according to Vladimir, made them lose interest, and they left the fair right away. Afterward, with this family obligation out of the way and thanks to Gallimard publishers, Irina and he could see each other every day. Vladimir had to negotiate the publication of *Despair*, which was going to be his first novel translated from English into French. Vladimir himself had done the translation into English with the help of an experienced English editor. The negotiation with the publishers gave him a pretext to leave home and meet Irina.

Inevitably, their time together came to an end. Afterward she would take the Métro home, and he would walk to his next appointment at the Café de Flore: The poet Jules Supervielle and the writer and artist Henri Michaux would be waiting for him there. He and Irina said their farewells in front of the modernist Métro station of

Saint-Michel. He repeated that everything would work out and they would see each other again; it was only a question of time, they had to be patient. Since Vladimir gave no hint of planning to leave his family, she didn't ask what would be arranged, nor how. She didn't ask because she didn't want to destroy their last moment together. Afterward, she reproached herself for not having questioned him about his plans. And that, in fact, was the reason she had traveled to Cannes.

When he set off with his family for the Côte d'Azure, he wrote her often at first, and every letter was a ray of light in the darkness of her solitude, but then more and more time passed between his letters. She wrote a poem about the subject, and after thinking about it long and hard, sent it to him.

Vladimir's words of love sounded emptier and emptier until they seemed quite dead. Perhaps a deep despondency lay behind them, Irina told herself. More and more often, he begged her to forgive him; he told her that there were many reasons why he was writing less often. At last, he asked her to stop writing him letters "temporarily." When he finally told her that his wife had discovered that they kept on writing to each other, his house had become a hell. She offered to go to Cannes so that they could go away together...forever. He wrote her back immediately, saying for God's sake, don't do it. But in spite of all that, she went; she needed to find out if she had any hope left. And, although he forbade it, she sent another letter, including some verses from the poet Polonsky:

He trembled and whispered in my ear:
"Listen, we will run away!
We will be free as the birds."

No answer at all came from Cannes.

The church bells had just rung four thirty. The sun, which was beginning to set, reached the bench where Irina was sitting. She got up. There was no point in waiting any longer. The voice on the beach that had arranged a meeting in the park must have been a hallucination.

With her bathing suit and her towel, she sat down on the beach in the same place where she had laid down that morning. She would give anything to see him again! But neither he nor his family were there, and their towels had disappeared. She walked up and down the beach, letting the waves bathe her feet. It was pleasant... as if the water wanted to make up for what Vladimir had denied her. She walked along, self-absorbed, but never forgetting for even a minute that he might be nearby. Although she didn't see him, he might be watching her. She felt as though she were on a set; she didn't dare commit the slightest error for fear of letting down her invisible audience.

5

In the meantime, after lunch and a nap, he had left home with Véra and Mitia. They crossed the park and entered the tunnel underneath the tracks. The noise of the train resounded overhead. After eating, he had felt unable

to write. He could not get Irina out of his head. He had
wanted to meet her, but it was impossible. The storm at
home had not died down, and Véra kept watching him.
No matter how hard the two of them tried to be considerate of each other, the marriage was still tense. He had
to be careful and play his part. For Véra, who knew him
as well as she knew herself, he was transparent. She saw
everything.

When they came out of the tunnel, the sun blinded
him. A man selling ice cream was passing by on the beach.
Vladimir offered a big one to Mitia, in order to give himself
time to get his bearings.

"I want a scoop of strawberry and another of lemon,"
the boy begged.

"I'll have just a scoop of vanilla," Véra said with a smile.
"And what do you want, Volodia? I can see you have your
head in the clouds again."

"I'm thinking over the next chapter in my head. You
know what I'm like," he said, trying to keep his irritation
from showing.

At that point, he glimpsed Irina making her way along
the beach, graceful and long-legged, picking up shells and
sinking her feet in the sand, between the waves.

"Papa, Papa, don't you hear us?"

"Volodia, which ice cream do you want?"

Irina stood still against the background of the sea. He
saw her eyes. It seemed as though someone had driven two
little holes in her head so that he could see the turquoise
waves through them. Yes, that's what it was like! Her eyes

were exactly the same color as the Mediterranean just before sunset.

Then he answered, "Me? I want raspberry as usual."

He was annoyed that Véra was bothering him about something as silly as an ice-cream cone.

Véra headed to their usual spot, spread out the towels, and Mitia went to erect a sandcastle where the waves were bathing the shore. Vladimir left him alone. Irina went over to the boy and his castle.

"Volodia, I want to sunbathe a while in peace," said Véra, finishing her little ice cream. "Go play with Mitia a while, keep an eye on him."

"I will, I will, but let me finish my ice cream. The boy is right here. Nothing is going to happen to him."

"Of course, but I'd rest easier if…"

Véra didn't finish her sentence. She lay facedown on the towel and exposed her back to the sun.

Irina got as far as the first wall of the castle Mitia was building and smiled at the little boy. Oddly, he made a face at her before returning her smile. She circled around the castle and sat on her towel a little way off. Vladimir gave her a look of gratitude, but she was focusing on the waves that came close and then rolled back out without touching her. She was deep in thought. Vladimir went over to Mitia and, with his back to Irina, helped him finish his sandcastle. It was the best way to handle the confusion caused by having her within sight. He tried to concentrate on the game. It did not take them long to build a Gothic castle with four towers, all of them complete with walls, bridges, and crenellation.

"Mama, look! Here are the dungeons," shouted Mitia, excited to be showing his mother one of the towers. "And here's the stable where they keep the horses. Can you hear them whinnying? Mine is the one with the white mane!"

A chilly wind began to blow, and Véra started putting her things in a big bag. The beach emptied out quickly. Vladimir did not let himself look back until they had gone some distance on the promenade. Then he looked at the beach avidly. Irina was still sitting there, looking at the sea with her head bent down. Full of longing, disconsolate, Vladimir examined for the last time that long neck with the rounded nape that was lost bit by bit in her short, curly hair. He realized there would be no other dates between them and tried to engrave that image on his memory. Yes, it would be the last time.

6

She let her feet carry her away and wound up at the lighthouse. Once she was there, she sat down and looked at the sea, wondering if she had made some mistake while she went over the time before they first met. She had been anxious to meet that attractive writer who stood out from the others, like a solitary poplar in the middle of a field. In fact, they had met a year before during his first visit to Paris. Afterward, he had written her a few times, but most of them were letters written to her and her mother. Irina was convinced that he had been inspired by her when he wrote "Spring in Fialta," a story about an amazing femme fatale. He insisted that he had written it before meeting her, but Irina didn't believe him. In the story, the woman was depicted as someone who influences men's destinies, and that was the way she saw herself. She didn't give much importance to the fact that Vladimir was married. He had never pretended to be single, and, in any event, she knew he was married before she met him. He had told her he was happily married, but she believed in the power of love. She analyzed it all again now, remembering the conversation they had had that morning. She thought of something she must not have wanted to see, something she should have said straight out but had failed to.

Someone sat down by her side. She didn't want to see who it was. She felt it was Vladimir, could sense his presence. Having him close by calmed her down, as it always had. But no. He wasn't sitting beside her. He would never be beside her again. Their affair had ended.

It was getting dark. The sun had set a good while ago, and the sea had a violet tinge. She heard the jingle of bells and turned her head. Once again it was the little donkey with the red hooves: The Queen of Ice Cream. The animal must be heading home, where it would eat its fill of hay and lie down. Everyone was heading home. She was the only one who didn't know what to do. The sleepwalker. She got up, stroked the donkey's mane, and made for downtown. To the station. But before she got there, she turned onto a narrow street on the right and found herself on the little square that gave her a view of his window. Night had fallen while she was walking.

"I need to know what cards I have to play," she thought. Vladimir had always told her to wait, to be patient, that everything would get better, that he couldn't live without her. But he clearly couldn't live without his wife and his son either. He needed to make up his mind. She should tell him why she had come. Yes, she should go to his house, knock on the door, introduce herself, and tell all of them why she had come. This would automatically lead to a conclusion.

There was light in only one window. The three bathing suits were once again hung out on the line: his, hers, and the child's. A table lamp illuminated the interior, and its yellowish light shone on the wall and the table. No one was in the room. After a little while, the light grew dim. A figure was blocking it. Irina saw, in front of the lighted lamp, the dark silhouette of a slender woman.

At that moment, she turned around and left without looking back. She had reached her goal. She knew what cards she held. The conclusion had been decided on its own.

III

NOCTURNE

VÉRA

New York–Boston, 1964

1

When she reached the Metropolitan Opera, Véra took off her mink coat; it had a wide collar like a shawl. Filippa helped her and afterward took off her own coat, a white gabardine that was suitable for spring weather. Both women joined the line of people who were holding the lightweight, colorful coats they wanted to check in the cloakroom. The happy murmur of the crowd showed that, along with the change in the weather, a carefree mood full of expectations had arrived. During the trip from Boston to New York, Véra had commented that at long last it seemed the weather was becoming more reasonable. Véra and Filippa left the cloakroom counter holding the metal tokens with their numbers. The opera would begin in twenty-five minutes.

"Should we have a drink to help us recuperate from the trip, Miss Rolf?"

Filippa laughed in amusement at Véra's formal manner. It was as if she wanted every gesture and word to show that—after her husband's literary success and a year in Europe—she had changed and was now a cut above the rest of them.

"I'd love to, Véra." Even though she was speaking to a woman from an older generation, Filippa used her first name in the American fashion. "After driving from Boston to New York, we deserve a good drink."

While they made their way through the crowd, all in formal dress, with high heels, patent leather shoes, and black dress suits, Filippa thought again with surprise that Véra had returned to the United States in the spring wearing a fur coat. She had seen the consternation Véra evoked at Harvard. After a year in Switzerland, her American friends hardly recognized her. For all the years she had lived in America, Véra had always worn black, lightweight coats no matter how cold the weather. Now her friends were shocked to see that when she came back with her husband for a short literary tour, she was dressing like a rich woman, with pearls and a mink that shone under the spring sun like the coat of a racehorse. Filippa, a Swede, knew that fur coats like Véra's drew attention and that North American intellectuals only used them in icy weather and with discretion. The sort of ostentatious luxury Véra exhibited now would strike them as the affectation of someone newly rich. Showing off had no place in their scale of values.

2

"The Countess of Almaviva, that's you, Véra," Filippa whispered in the half-light of the opera.

The Countess of Almaviva appeared on the set holding herself very upright and looking impressive in her white wig and the vague half smile of a woman who is suffering even though she is too proud to admit it and tries to hide it behind her title and her magnificent appearance. The soprano Lisa Della Casa was one of the stars in that night's performance of *The Marriage of Figaro*. Almaviva, the countess's husband, was played by Dietrich Fischer-Dieskau.

Véra and Filippa, a doctoral student at Harvard, had gone to New York for the debut. Even though it was a five-hour drive, Véra was determined to attend because that night Dmitri would replace Peter Lagger, who was sick. She planned to return to Harvard the next day for a reading Vladimir was scheduled to give. Filippa would stay on in New York to finish some research at the New York Public Library. Véra didn't remember what it was about—something or other to do with the Swedish poets. She gave it no importance.

Filippa turned toward Véra again, looked at her, and whispered something in her ear. Véra shook her head indignantly. On her lips the cold half smile of the Mona Lisa appeared.

"Had you never really thought about it, Véra? I can't believe it!" Filippa insisted with the audacity of the young. It could be charming, but it bothered Véra just then.

Filippa's breath quickened. The idea interested her. She was wearing a maroon velvet dress. Véra was wearing the silk dress she always wore for serious occasions. Her thick, white hair, her milky skin, and a long pearl necklace doubled around her neck contrasted with the black outfit. When she got dressed, Véra had thought of the cold, full moon in the sky at night.

The charming Lisa Della Casa sang the countess's famous aria, "Porgi, amor." Filippa had not meant to offend Véra. The countess was a magnificent, lively woman. She had not realized that Mozart was not one of Véra's favorite composers, far from it. He was too ethereal and insubstantial for her taste. She preferred things to be clear. As she saw it, his plots treated all moral values as relative, and this went against her principles.

The concert hall erupted in applause. Véra felt they were applauding for her.

During the recitative, Filippa whispered, "On first sight, she looks like an angel. Like Lisa Della Casa, who is an angel."

Véra was surprised by that, since it was an opinion she did not share. She half smiled and thought to herself, "No, I am not the Countess of Almaviva, whose husband is notorious for seducing women. I am a successful woman to whom her husband owes his fame."

Filippa continued, "But she is the Angel of Destruction."

Véra was ready to take offense, but Filippa would not permit her interruption. "Or a wolf. She has the profile of a wolf and the clear, gray eyes of a wolf."

Véra began to suspect that she was transparent and that Filippa saw through her. Sleepwalkers tend to do that. She stood up. She hadn't realized that the recitative had ended and that Cherubino, played by the mezzo soprano Tatiana Troyanos, was now singing her aria, "Voi che sapete che cosa é amor." Yes, the wolf's mask she had worn years ago for the party in Berlin...

3

...she was just over twenty and had read Vladimir's verses over and over until she had learned them by heart.

Like every other woman, she wanted to meet the author. Her father had invited him a number of times to his publishing house in Berlin, where Véra was working, but almost as if it were intentional, she was never there when he came. She was hoping to see him at the dance given by the Russian emigrants, hoping for a chance to meet him. She thought that she could only attract a special man like him by doing something original. That's why she had chosen to wear not a delicate, feminine mask but the head of a wolf.

At the dance, she saw that Vladimir was looking for someone. Véra followed him like his shadow, waiting for the right moment. The night was offering her a chance, and she did not intend to lose it. She never wasted an opportunity. In spite of her youth, she understood very clearly that life will not give us more than one chance. Véra knew that Vladimir was looking for Svetlana, the woman who had just left him. The ghetto of Russians in Berlin held no secrets. Seeing that he hadn't found Svetlana and that he did not show much enthusiasm for his dancing partners, still disguised in her wolf mask, she walked by him at a distance that would allow him to admire her slender figure.

When he asked her to dance, she pretended not to know who he was, and she did not take off the mask even when he asked her to. She knew that her mask was provocative, and she feared that he, who was accustomed to Svetlana's beauty, would distain her bony face behind the wolf mask. Filippa had said it clearly. She realized that Vladimir was imagining a stunning woman. With her face covered, she felt like that. But only with her face covered.

They left the dance to stroll through the Berlin night. It was the eighth of May, Vladimir insisted although she thought it was the ninth. A few trees were blooming, but she no longer remembered their smell. The dim light of the sleeping city favored her plan. She wanted the mask to stay snug on her face so that she would never again have to show her nose. She knew all about male vanity, so she recited his own verses back to him. First, she chose a love poem but saw immediately that it was a bad choice. The author began to picture the woman who had inspired it. After that, she recited a poem about a mirror, and another about a fast train. She saw right away that with those choices, she had surpassed Svetlana. She added two other long poems, which she recited slowly and with emotion. He reproached her, laughing, claiming her recital sounded like a drama teacher and then, seeing he had hurt her with his sarcasm, he praised the way she pronounced the vowels. The praise hurt her even more than the reproach, but she covered her unhappiness with a half smile. He kept her company up to her front door and then carefully took off her mask. She felt exposed, wondering what impression her face—as crooked as a cubist painting—would make on that expert in female beauty.

She was well aware that, a little later, when Vladimir went to France to work on the farm in Provence, he was only thinking about the girl who had abandoned him. He wrote his first letters to her. His memories of Svetlana made Vladimir indifferent to other stimuli, and he did not respond to Véra's letters. She had to write three times, no,

four, to get a single response from him. But she had made
her plan, and she was determined to win him over. The task
would not be easy, because he had raised a wall of indifference between them. Yet the cooler he was to her, the more
insistent she became. In public, Véra acted as though she
knew nothing about the situation. To screw up her courage, she hummed from the aria in *Carmen*, "*et si je t'aime
prends garde à toi*," knowing she was not remotely like the
bewitching Carmen.

At that moment, the tall, slim gardener appeared on
the set. It was Dmitri! Yes, it was Mitia, who was on fire,
singing his aria to Count Almaviva. Dressed as he was, she
hardly recognized him, and it was very strange to hear him
sing Mozart. She heard him sing, and he seemed like someone else. Wagner, Tchaikovsky, those were the right composers for her son, but to hear him sing an aria as delicate
as a spider's web...

Véra had been ambitious from a very young age. She
wanted to do something great with her life although she
didn't know what. She knew she didn't have any artistic
talent and lacked creative genius. She took a stab at literary translation. She made a real effort; her translations
were correct...but nothing more. There was nothing in
them to criticize, but they lacked life and the spirit that
creators have in abundance, so she decided to realize the
work of her life by creating someone whom she could help
by fusing with him and becoming part of his creation, but
she had not found anyone with that sort of talent. No
scientist, no painter, much less a musician or writer. Until

the day she read the poetry that in those days Vladimir signed under the pseudonym of Sirin and realized that he was what she had been looking for. She went to a reading in a bookstore given by that poet, that brilliant young man who encompassed everything she was lacking: as happy as a child during summer vacation, as light as a tennis ball, as lively as the butterflies that flew out of his verses. And thanks to Véra's legendary obstinance, they had been together for more than forty years. She remembered how complicated the years had been with that playful creator, and sighed so deeply that the man in the row ahead of her rubbed his hand over the nape of his neck.

Yes, Vladimir was as frisky and as happy as a kitten, something that irritated her, that distracted her from the important questions of life. Once, in a Parisian hotel, he had found a Finish-French dictionary left by another guest. Vladimir sat down comfortably in the armchair with that dictionary and began to read it amid gales of laughter.

"In Finish, 'telephone' is *puhelin.* Can you imagine? 'Airport' is *lentoasema*...the foreigners will never find it! 'Sierra' is *tunturi*; 'mountain,' *järti*; 'lagoon,' *lampi*; and 'sacred'—watch out—it's *pyhä!*"

Véra reminded him that he was about to have an interview with a journalist and that he should be gearing up for it, but he kept on laughing at the word *retheilymaya*, that apparently meant "tavern." Véra couldn't take any more, and she tore the dictionary from his hands. He loved nothing better than to play and to joke. It had meant a lot of work for her, keeping him on target for the work he needed to do.

Trying not to make any noise unwrapping it, she accepted the chocolate Filippa was offering her. On the stage, Susanna and the Countess of Almaviva sang an insipid little duet.

She had discovered Vladimir's weakness for women a long time ago, for women who were young and women who were not so young but more refined. It was hard to deal with. Like the countess, she had had to come up with different rattraps to catch him. She knew that in Russian circles, people said that Véra had coerced Vladimir into marrying her. They may have been right, but... so what? We all create our own lives. If she hadn't organized it, he wouldn't have married her, and with a different wife, he would never have become a famous writer. From the start, she had insisted on total transparency between them. She made him write a diary in the same notebook she used to jot down her thoughts. In that way, she controlled every thought that crossed his mind. She learned to decipher the notes written in a purposely illegible hand, like ciphers not intended for her eyes. She knew that he wrote down his memories of Lyussya and Svetlana, and later his memories of Irina, and, finally, of Katherine, and his dreams about all four of them. Although he pretended to know nothing about them, he still had not forgotten them. Since his episode with that damned nymph Irina, Véra understood very clearly that she could not take any more risks. That's why she accompanied him to his classes at the American universities as an assistant and waited for him in front of the student union when class had ended to drive him home, far from the temptation of those girls who were lurking everywhere on campus.

At that moment, the countess was singing the aria "Dove sono i belli momenti." What had become of the beautiful moments with her husband, who only had eyes for other women and humiliated his countess, who wanted her husband for herself. Véra knew all about that. Filippa was right. She identified so intensely with the aria that it gave her gooseflesh. And she decided not to wait until the next day but instead to return to Boston that same night.

4

From the car she saw a long bridge in front of her, crossing a river. It shone in the darkness of the night. She didn't understand how she could have taken a wrong turn and wound up at that enormous bridge. Between Manhattan and Boston she did not have to cross any wide rivers and even less after she had passed the Saw Mill. The sign announced "Tappan Zee Bridge." Véra realized that the bridge must cross the Hudson. Faced with a choice of various destinations, she finally decided on Sleepy Hollow because it sounded familiar. Once she got there, she parked in a square and realized that she had only advanced a few miles. At this rate, who knew when she would reach Boston. She got out of the car to stretch her legs and breathed in the spring air. In front of her was a hotel with a lighted green sign that read "The Headless Horseman" and, on the right, a bar that announced in red "Washington Irving."

She headed toward the bar and from the darkness saw a few night owls who, half asleep, were having the last drink of the evening. Suddenly, she realized she was in Sleepy Hollow, where Washington Irving's story about the Headless Horseman was set, a place where supernatural happenings are natural. In spite of disdaining Irving and his fantastical world, she felt a chill: What if she had gotten lost, because the place drew her? "How silly," she chided herself. "Think!" Wouldn't she do well to take the pill Filippa had given her just in case. She entered the bar and asked the barman for a glass of water.

"Wouldn't you like me to fix you a daiquiri, ma'am? Or a black Russian? Or maybe a margarita? Leave the water to the animals!"

The martini glass that held the daiquiri smelled of lime and rum, and Véra tried it with pleasure. It was refreshing; it would help her pull herself together again. She took the pill with water and after that drank the tasty cocktail. She left a considerable tip for the barman and thanked him for giving her good advice.

After that, she found the highway that led to Hartford by way of Danbury and left the state of New York behind.

5

Once she had left Sleepy Hollow, the car trip went fast until, by mistake, she left the highway and wound up on a bumpy road blanketed under a spring snowstorm, which would probably be the last of the season, since it was April now. There was no place to turn the enormous Chevrolet around. Where she rented the car, they had only had big models. Véra would have preferred something smaller, a sports car, for instance. She thought about Volodia: She would have to remind him to be sure to read the end of *Lolita* when he gave his reading the next day at the Sanders Theatre at Harvard. These were the pages in which we see Lolita's husband and his friends as Americans who have been injured in the Second World War while Lolita's seducer, a European, has survived undamaged in the United States, well clear of a war provoked by the Europeans. Not just that, but he has devoted his time to seducing little girls. That passage would go over well at the university. The students and academics were always interested in leftist-leaning social themes. Véra made a face: Those were issues that, fortunately, Volodia didn't take up often. "Don't forget," she told herself while she continued through the bright, snowy landscape that offset the darkness of the night. No, she would not forget to tell him.

The pill Filippa had given her was working wonderfully. Véra felt fresh, and she concentrated on the road even though she didn't know where it would lead her. Suddenly, she saw a sign for Wolcott, Connecticut. She would continue straight on. Filippa always observed everything, always judged everything. In the café, where they had drunk champagne and eaten canapés with Dmitri after the opera, Filippa's eyes were glued to the little beaded black bag that Véra carried. Filippa was always obsessed with disguises.

How did they meet each other, Véra wondered at the same time that she read a sign for the next town: Bristol, Connecticut. And how could she figure out which way to go? She saw a silo and next to it a house, but the lights were off. She answered: It was all her fault. In 1960 an unknown Swedish poet had written to ask if it would be possible for them to meet sometime. Véra thought she might find someone who could translate Vladimir's work into Swedish. Not just that, she might help them escape from the clutches of the editors, who were making things difficult for Vladimir, and recommend a different editor. She told Volodia, in Cannes, that a brilliant young poet wanted to meet them.

"What should we do?" Vladimir asked carefully so she wouldn't notice that he was dying to meet the young woman.

"See her. At least we'll have some fun. Why not?" she answered, pretending not to care.

Filippa came to Nice. Vladimir tested her with a number of questions. Filippa answered easily, and they invited her to have dinner with them in the Negresco, the famous luxury hotel.

Once they had chosen the first course and the wine, Vladimir said in a dreamy way that made Véra think he was joking, "When I was a child, I used to eat dinner here with my parents when we were on vacation."

"That would have been quite a trick," Filippa corrected him. "Back then, the hotel didn't even exist."

"She has paid him back with the same coin," Véra thought, annoyed with Filippa. She could not bear anyone to contradict her husband.

Vladimir blushed because it seemed as though he'd been caught out in a lie. However, he wasn't lying, he had dreamed up his stay at the hotel. He remembered perfectly well that he had spent summer vacations with his parents in Biarritz on the French Basque coast.

There was another road sign illuminated by the car's lights: Burlington. This meant nothing to Véra. It started to snow again. She kept going.

Filippa spent fifteen days with them in Nice. When she left, they were both exhausted, Véra remembered. She helped them with the Swedish editors and started to translate *Pale Fire* into Swedish, but after her departure she sent letters constantly as if their friendship gave her the right to endless, sentimental declarations. "I only have you two, and you mean so much to me," she wrote. In her response, Véra suggested that she show more restraint. They offered her an opportunity to study for her doctorate at Harvard.

Véra knew that after the success of *Lolita* she had changed: She didn't waste time with people, not even when they could be useful. Vladimir was different; the situation amused him. He had said not long ago that life was like a carnival, a masquerade ball as long as you knew how to see it that way. Why had Filippa mentioned repeatedly the theme of the disguise? "Véra, when are you going to take off your mask?" Volodia reminded her recently that from the time they had met at the costume ball, she had never taken off her wolf's face.

She drove through the snowstorm thinking that, in the café, Filippa had looked closely at her purse. Véra suspected that she had divined the contents. So she hid the purse in her lap, under the table.

It had stopped snowing, and the snow on the road was melting. In the darkness, she saw a dim light and drove toward it. It was a gas station. A man in an orange jacket and a hood was standing outside as if he were waiting for her and singing "Orange Colored Sky." She almost thought it was Nat King Cole himself, and she was embarrassed to ask for help, but she overcame her reluctance and asked him to fill the tank and clean the windshield. He made a recommendation: "Don't go through Hartford, ma'am. I would go through Springfield. It's closer and the road is better. It will turn light soon, and you should get to Boston in about three hours."

Véra paid him and thanked him. He answered, "Okay," and started singing: "Perhaps, perhaps, perhaps." He sang with a strong American accent to the wind that smelled of spring.

6

At the same time, Dmitri was drawing close to the St. Regis, the hotel where he was staying and where he had invited Filippa to have a drink in the magnificent King Cole Bar. After the opera, all three had given toasts, but neither of the women had referred to his performance or to the opera. It had been a little odd. Later he had asked his mother where she would be spending the night.

"I'm not staying. I've decided to go back to Boston right away."

"Now? At night? It's crazy. You'll fall asleep on the road."

"Enough, Mitia. You know I'm not going to change my mind. Tomorrow night your father has an important event at Harvard."

"We can set off together early," Filippa interjected. "At six, for example. We'll be there by eleven at the latest."

"It's late. Volodia will need me as soon as he gets up."

Filippa took out a little crystal bottle from her purse and emptied two yellowish tablets on the table.

"Véra, take these with you. They will help you get there safely. You won't fall asleep, and you'll be calm. I take them every day."

"Thank you." Véra thought a minute and then asked, "Why do you take them?"

"I suffer from bouts of anxiety that alternate with a sense of euphoria that's so intense it's unbearable. This medicine is...a miracle pill."

"I would go with you, Mama, but tomorrow morning we have rehearsal," Dmitri said. "Reserve a room in my hotel. Or I'll ask them to put another bed in my room. For many years, we slept together. Remember?"

"Yes, and your father worked in the next room until late at night. But, no, Mitia. I'll reach Boston and Harvard in four hours. There won't be any traffic at night, and I'm a wild beast on the road."

"Don't forget to take the pill," Filippa insisted. "Here's a glass of water. And take the other one with you just in case."

When Véra opened her black purse to put the pill there, Filippa examined it again, thinking that for an evening bag, it seemed very heavy.

7

On the way to the St. Regis, Dmitri pictured his mother driving at night through various states and the cities of Middletown, Hartford, and Worcester until she reached Boston, her back perfectly erect, her eyes wide open and fixed on the road. He admired her, but then thought of what had happened when he went with her to get her car. Since she was wearing high heels, they walked along Fifth Avenue as if they were taking a stroll. A woman of about fifty stopped to look at her, and Dmitri thought she must be sizing up Véra's mink coat and perhaps even wondering how much it was worth. When they had almost passed her, the woman, who was wearing a thin red coat, exclaimed, "It's you, Véra. How have you been?"

It was Jenni Moulton, a German married to an American teacher. She explained that she too had left Cornell: Her husband had accepted a position teaching at Princeton. Véra told her that Dmitri had performed in a Mozart opera at the Metropolitan. Jenni remembered that he had studied singing, and she congratulated him. Dmitri had not forgotten her either. She had changed very little from the time he knew them, the woman and her husband, at the suppers the group of friends enjoyed in Cornell. He remembered Jenni had played chess with him in his room. Once she had joined him for a game while Véra was holding forth on Proust. Jenni must have felt, as he did, that his mother not only wanted to share her ideas about her reading but also to impress her guests and her husband. Dmitri liked Jenni in part because of the sense of complicity they shared that night.

"In California, I thought about you every day, Mrs. Moulton," Véra told her.

Jenni, who was happy to have run into them, showed her surprise. "That's wonderful, but I have no idea why you thought about me every day."

"Oh, my dear, it's because in Hollywood, we had a German maid," Véra answered coldly.

8

The ice queen, Dmitri thought, with those pale eyes that took on an almost fanatical light when she saw his father. The goddess of winter with her hair the color of frost and her skin as white as snow, on which time had engraved its delicate designs like the ice on glass windowpanes.

He thought again about his mother and his father when they had people over to eat. From the time he was little, he had been aware of his mother's attachment to his father as if she were living his life and not her own. She defended his opinions vehemently, and if Vladimir started to argue, even when it was with someone as close to him as Edmund Wilson, Véra immediately fell upon his opponent. Dmitri knew that Véra was too affected and "square" for Wilson's taste and that most people could not bear her sarcasm or her arrogance. She liked virtually no other living author because she recognized only the superior genius of her husband. It was very clear in their family: His father was the genius, and no one could compete with him. That's why Dmitri had chosen another field: As a singer he could not be compared to his father.

His mother had changed in recent years. Since the huge success of *Lolita*, she had developed a taste for luxury, which had not remotely interested her in the past. He would never have thought she had that inclination. His father was indifferent to her predilections. He was only interested in being left alone to write. He even smiled when, on their first European reading tour—at the time, they were still traveling from the United States, their home, to Europe, and not the other way around—they traveled with ten trunks. His only interest was his work, and he left his wife alone. When they stopped in Nice on that trip, Dmitri spent a week with them. They stayed in an apartment with eight ample rooms on the Promenade des Anglais, no less, with magnificent views. Dmitri remembered his first impression. Their windows looked out on the turquoise sea and the sky where scattered clouds and patches of fog floated by. The apartment was furnished in Louis XV style, and the walls were covered with paintings that were, albeit a little battered, at least from the period.

"How fancy!" he exclaimed.

"But Mitia, you can't be serious! Because of a couple of junk-shop finds!" she said, opening her arms. "Luxury is something else altogether, but since you're a bohemian, what do you know?" she scolded him, before adding in English, "Fancy, my foot!"

What had become of the solicitous mother who had raised him in rented rooms or tiny apartments with cheap furniture and sometimes even without furniture in Berlin, in Paris, and later in New York and at the American universities? He had never seen her wearing expensive fur coats, or long ropes of real pearls, or gold, or fancy hairdos styled by expensive hairdressers. Of course, they hadn't had the money to do that before, so Dmitri could never have suspected his mother's secret longings. It was true that she had often complained about the shortage of money and sometimes reproached his father for not making more. Vladimir had asked her then to accept their hardships with a smile instead of complaints. In the café at the opera house, Filippa, whose openness was likable, had told her, "You are like a beautiful embellishment for the armchair, Véra."

The real meaning lay in the word "like." Without that little word, with a bit of imagination, the sentence could have been seen as praise, but that "like" implied a touch of criticism. Filippa was right. Luckily, Véra didn't realize it. English was not her mother tongue so she took it as praise and reacted with the slight smile of one of the beautiful women in a Maupassant novel.

His father had always been philosophical about it. Dmitri remembered him as short-tempered only when he had first begun to write in English. He was writing a mysterious book then that was only whispered about at home and that turned out to be *Lolita*. Every day he bought the newspapers that followed the case of a young girl who had been kidnapped by a much older man, who drove her all over the United States. His father threw things around and stationed himself by an open window to smoke cigarette after cigarette even though his doctor had forbidden it. He also secretly drank wine straight from the bottle and sometimes he even emptied the refrigerator. He prowled around the house like a caged lion and muttered that his metaphors sounded tortured and rigid in English, anything but natural. And he repeated constantly that if he couldn't write in Russian, he would let it all go to hell and burn his manuscript.

He didn't burn it, although he tried. Véra stopped him. The neighbor told Dmitri later that he had seen his father set a fire in a metal wastebasket and then throw in the pile of papers that was the manuscript he had worked on so hard. Véra got there soon after, opened her eyes wide, pulled the manuscript out of the fire, and stomped on the burning pages to put out the fire. Apparently, his father watched the scene with a scowl. His mother caught the pages in her arms like a pastry she had just taken out of the oven—although she never baked pastries; Dmitri had only seen cakes at his friends' birthday parties. She put the pages in the bottom drawer of the chest, locked it with a key, and put the key in her pocket.

Soon after came the phase when his mother became bad-tempered and intransigent. They would soon have to pay his tuition at the university, and it was not at all clear they could manage. When he was fifteen, he assured his mother that when he finished high school, he would become a mountain climber, and that he might not even have to finish high school. He would become a mountain climber right away and would earn enough to take care of his family.

His father came back from class and told his mother that he loved her even when she was mean to him, but that when she smiled at him, he loved her even more. However, she didn't smile, and his father complained that she was constantly whining about money. Why didn't she find a job? Dmitri knew how she would respond because not working was one of the rules of the aristocracy, especially among the women, and she, a daughter of the bourgeoisie, wanted to act like an aristocrat even though her husband and their American friends were totally indifferent to such foolery.

Fortunately, his mother's outbursts didn't bother Dmitri. He remembered a summer when, still a teenager, he was with his parents in Vermont at some friends' house. He wrote a sort of story there about a mother who was so good to her son that, on the one hand, when she was going to scold him, she made him take laughing gas. On the other hand, however, she forbade him to read the obligatory assignments. He remembered *The Adventures of Tom Sawyer*, a book that, according to his mother, was not appropriate reading for kids. His mother even went to talk to the teacher and explained why she objected to the book on moral grounds. They didn't understand her, and because of her rigidity, Dmitri got a bad grade in literature. The Russian word *printsipialnost*, a question of principles, was the order of the day in their house.

His mother must have reached Stanford or New Haven, but the greater part of the drive still lay ahead of her. He could have driven her to Harvard the next day right after his rehearsal and also attended his father's reading. He would have enjoyed it. But instead of waiting, his mother, who was so hardheaded, had taken off into the night. At the same time, he was proud of her for having undertaken the trip on her own, with champagne in her head and a mysterious pill in her veins. When he got back to Milan, he would buy himself a sports car. He already knew which one: a Triumph TR3. He would be as aggressive a pilot as she was. He wanted to be like that crazy, marvelous sleepwalker who was his mother.

9

Filippa was waiting for Dmitri in the hotel bar. She was sitting under the enormous modernist mural by Maxfield Parrish, and the orange colors of the mural reflected on her face. She was drinking sparkling rosé. Dmitri thought it matched the color of her dress and ordered the same thing: "Pink champagne, please!"

It was after midnight. People had settled into the dark corners of the bar and were slowly having their last drinks. Filippa told Dmitri that his mother had not been happy to find out that Filippa's Swedish partner had come to Harvard to be with her and that the two young women would live together.

"That's typical of my mother," Dmitri said, and laughed. "And I'm sure she made excuses for her anger by saying that your friend's company would distract you from your studies, no?"

"Exactly. Your father doesn't interfere with anything. He's like a butterfly that has escaped from his collection, that flies all about and gathers, like nectar, stories about us silly people," commented Filippa, laughing too and joining Dmitri in a toast.

"My mother has always been fussy about social norms, but that also has its value: A woman can't comment on a man's clothing even though it's fine for it to happen the other way around. A man can only kiss the hand of a married woman. I'll bet my father has never kissed you? If he had done, he would have heard from my mother. Sometimes all these social norms are a nuisance, but God help the person who tells her so!"

"And she can't bear professional women or women writers. She despises them."

"Except for you."

"You're wrong there. I didn't want to talk about that, but instead about both of your parents. They have absolutely no interest in practical things. Just the opposite. Daily life for them is taboo. They can only talk about art in capital letters and about their taste in literature. Three years ago, when I spent a couple of weeks—a long two weeks—in Nice (ah, I see you have heard about it!), I realized that they hardly tolerate any twentieth-century writers. As for the dead, they can only utter a few names: Flaubert, Pushkin and Gogol, Kafka, Proust and Joyce."

"My mother only believes in my father's talent. My uncle on my father's side is a great poet. My mother insulted him once when she asked him to translate my father's novels into Russian. But it's true: If she didn't believe so fanatically in my father, he would have had a hard time getting as far as he has, even harder as a foreigner. How did you put up with such a long visit in Nice?"

"I was a nervous wreck at the end of every day. They always disagreed with something, and they attacked all my literary and political convictions. Finally, I didn't know who I was or where I belonged."

"They took you in as though you were their daughter. So, in fact, we're brother and sister!" Dmitri said, toasting her with the rest of the champagne before ordering two more glasses. "Now you can see why I moved to Milan, far from America. But Mama won't let me get away. She is forcing my father to live in Montreux in the ostentatious Palace Hotel, which the old money she adores would despise so much they wouldn't even drink a cup of coffee there. As for my father, he loves America and only feels at home here, but she has him under control in that corner of the world because she has conquered it. Keeping him in Montreux is her vendetta against him. She's a Mafia boss."

"And a little Napoleon."

"De Gaulle!"

"Bismarck!"

"Mussolini! Did you know that she always carries a Browning?"

If Filippa was shocked, she hid it. "No, I didn't know, but she must have carried it today, and I don't doubt that it's loaded."

"You're spot-on."

"I wondered why her evening purse was so heavy. Now, I see. Tonight she reminded me of the Countess of Almaviva."

"There's a reason. She's shrewd, elegant, but also vulnerable."

"You know, I have the odd feeling that Véra is projecting her desires onto me. I'm sure that in the past she had literary ambitions, she told me so once. And she has organized my life so I'll become a famous writer. She has told me to stop writing in Swedish because 'there's no time for the little languages. From now on, you must write in English. And no poetry! Leave Stockholm and come to America!'"

"And she arranged for you to come to the States, right? She did the same thing with my father: He had to stop writing stories and give up any idea of poetry, because novels sell much better. My mother figured out that *Lolita* would create a scandal because of the theme and that all the attention it attracted would translate into prestige but—more than that—she realized it would become a huge commercial success, the kind of success she had wanted all her life."

"Are you serious?"

"I watched the whole thing play out. But I admire her. I won't reach anything like that kind of fame. I'm not sure I'd even want it."

"Me neither. Why can't I write in Swedish? I've stopped writing altogether. I'm living in America, but I don't know why. I don't even know where I want to live or where I belong."

"I have the same feeling. I'm a bass at La Scala in Milan, but my mother wants me to translate my father's work into Italian. She only believes in him." He sipped a little champagne and added almost to himself, "Maybe she's right. She's gotten the result she wanted."

Filippa leaned toward him, took hold of his hand, and said in a soft voice, "Don't say that, Dmitri. I beg you."

"In our family, you'll only win if you have my mother's support. Every family has its pillar, and she is ours."

Filippa thought again about Véra's purse, and she shivered.

10

Véra was speeding down the highway. She had crossed into Massachusetts and believed that she would reach Harvard at any moment. It was morning, but the sun had not yet risen and the countryside was wrapped in thick fog like torn cotton that let very little be seen. The driver kept on, upright in her seat. There was not a hint of fatigue on her face, and the foggy landscape had a calming effect. In any event, she did not pay much attention to it, because she was deep in thought.

Lolita...in five years she had retyped the novel five times. She had devoted long hours to it, sometimes twelve a day. Another woman could not have borne such a life. Vladimir only lived when he was writing. She had driven him to it. Véra knew that, in his novels, her husband envisaged another sort of life for himself, the kind of life he might have led if he had taken another path. Usually it involved another woman, someone he had known before he met her or even during their marriage. But she had her secrets too. When she typed up his manuscripts, she looked for the best words, the most appropriate adjectives, and she substituted her own linguistic finds for his sometimes insufficient vocabulary in English. She was proud to leave her own mark, although it was small and anonymous, on world literature.

She saved the manuscript of *Lolita* when Vladimir, desperate because he couldn't write what he had in mind, tried to destroy it by throwing it into a wastebasket to which he had set fire.

"We'll keep it," was the only thing Véra said.

Even when the two of them had entered their sixties, she controlled Vladimir's every move and knew everything about him, like the mother of a child who is starting high school. She kept him away from women. A few years ago, in Hollywood, when Vladimir was writing the screenplay for *Lolita* with Stanley Kubrick, the dazzling Marilyn Monroe was interested in him and invited the two of them to have dinner at her Hollywood villa. Véra saw that in front of her Volodia showed off, charming Marilyn with his wit and his gift for satire. The actress—who appreciated such qualities— was dazzled. So, they wound up turning down the invitation in spite of Vladimir's protests. Véra called Marilyn in person to excuse them. All her life she'd been longing for Vladimir to grow old, to lose his appeal. Now she had him where she wanted him: shut up in a corner far away from the world. At the wheel, Véra sat up even straighter.

She had become essential to him some time ago. Without her, Vladimir could hardly exist. She was the only one who could read his fragmented style. No professional secretary would know how to advise him on the syntax of his work. Véra rejected literary agents to preserve her privacy and Vladimir's and also to keep anyone from finding out about certain episodes in his life. There had been a few. Vladimir had had more than one affair, and Véra had looked the other way; that is, until Irina came on the scene. Vladimir's romance with that Parisian Russian was a passion that shook her out of her usual state of somnolence. She opened her eyes and realized that anyone who wanted to defend something important would have to fight for it. That was almost thirty years ago.

Nearly thirty years ago, in the spring of the memorable year of 1937, Vladimir finally recognized that he had fallen in love with Irina. Véra would have preferred him to continue denying it. Yes, she had been convinced that her husband would abandon her. But she was determined not to give up. She didn't shout; she avoided that sort of vulgarity. Vladimir could not abide bad manners, hysteria, and pettiness. The only thing she did was tell him, with a half smile and an air of chilly condescension, to pack his bags and go. She would take Dmitri to America so that he, Vladimir, would never see him again. Afterward, she retreated into a silence so deep it was as if a thick veil covered her face. Vladimir saw only her indifference, the indescribable smile that had become part of her, and more than anything, her total lack of interest in what he did. He could not imagine how she felt, could not perceive her intention of saving her marriage, no matter what the cost. For Véra, that relationship was her whole life, and that's why she pretended not to care.

She knew that not only a man's love was at stake but also everything she wanted to achieve: to realize her great work through that hugely talented writer and never again to suffer the sensation of living without a goal.

Her threat of taking Mitia to live with her in the United States, mentioned in a low tone, as if casually, worked: In the end, Vladimir stayed with them. He stayed even though he suffered the loss of Irina. Véra noticed and said nothing. She only spoke about dull, everyday matters. She knew her husband thought many of the scenes in Dostoyevsky were exaggerated and vulgar. Véra did not act like Grushenka and even less like Nastasya Filippovna. She played the role of a good mother who gives all her love to her son and ignores her husband. It was as if he didn't exist in her eyes. At the same time, she began to dress and apply her makeup very carefully, making every effort to be elegant and irreproachable even though she knew Irina would best her in that competition. Here again, she was like the Countess of Almaviva, who will inevitably lose her husband's love to the fresh, capricious, passionate Susanna.

On the beach in Cannes, she realized that the solitary, dejected young woman who looked at them from time to time out of the corner of her eye could only be Irina. The girl was as supple as a serpent, as sensual as a cat. She also noticed that Vladimir approached her once and said something quickly, to arrange a date, she was sure. Véra was determined to circumvent his plans. All day she kept a close eye on him, like a dragon in fairy tales who locks up the beautiful princess. Vladimir invented one excuse after another to make his escape, but she was having none of it. He wouldn't go to the newspaper kiosk to buy cigarettes, and she wouldn't leave her post either. Instead, she sent little Mitia and then worried while he was gone although the kiosk was right there on the corner. Vladimir spent the whole afternoon trembling, his face pale: Once she caught him trying to sneak out the door, but she wouldn't allow it. She told herself again that if you want something badly, you have to fight for it. She had believed in that saying all her life. Volodia sat down at his desk, where his half-written novel waited, but he didn't go back to writing. Instead, he wept silently. She had never before seen him in such a pitiful state.

When night was falling, she saw the young woman from the beach on the dark street, looking toward their window. The girl could not see Véra, because the lamp was behind her. She could only make out a dark silhouette. She left soon after. A few months later, Véra forced Vladimir to ask Irina to send his letters back. It was essential: Véra had big plans for Vladimir's talent, and she could not let those letters appear in the future out of nowhere—the famous writer's letters to a lover who was not his wife. Vladimir objected, but after Véra repeated her threat of taking Mitia to parts unknown, he finally gave in. Véra dictated a letter to Irina in his name, and she mailed it herself. But, in spite of that effort, Irina never returned his letters.

From that time on, month after month, Véra bought a notebook in which the two of them together made daily records of their impressions. She had started the ritual earlier, but from the Irina episode on, she forced Volodia to write everything down with absolute regularity. She also controlled what he drank, because in his good moods he liked to drink. There was always something about him that was playful and irresponsible.

In the spring of that decisive year—1937—in Mariánské Lázně, Vladimir shut himself up in his room all day and locked the door. He was writing something. The story was titled "Cloud, Castle, Lake." He did not show it to Véra for a long time because, apparently, he had not finished it. In the United States, at the beginning of the forties, she urged him to finish it; it was one of the first stories he would publish. Before typing it up, Véra read it for the first time. It was a Kafkaesque story about Germany and the Germans, who denied the most basic freedoms to the individual and allowed even less to foreigners. When she typed it, instead of just transcribing what she saw, Véra examined the story carefully. The story she found spoke of something different: of a man named Vasily. The name started with V like Vladimir; in Russian the two names have an accent on the next to the last syllable and include the same vowels. They even rhyme with each other. Vasily lived between two realities: One was the usual kind, filled with obligations, all dark gray. The other reality, which he discovered during an outing, was perfect: Over a radiant, sky-blue lake, a great white cloud floated, and on the fresh green slope that led down to the lake, a stone castle reached up to the heavens. Vasily wanted to stay forever in the idyllic landscape, but he was not allowed to. Reality pulled him back from his dream; it tied him up hand and foot and forced him to return. As punishment, it beat him. Vasily became a downhearted man; he gave up his work. Life lost all meaning to him. Véra realized that she was the first reality, the gray one: a world in which there it was nothing left to discover. Everything there was ordinary, everyday, and full of unpleasant obligations. The excursion Vasily/Vladimir went on was the trip to Paris. The blue lake, Irina's eyes; the cloud, her curly blond hair; the green slope, her bearing and her fresh youthful manner; and the castle, her slim but strong figure. And, once again, the reality to which he was forced to return against his will was her, Véra.

11

The sun was shining down on the fields, which were starting to turn green again. There was no longer a trace of snow, and Véra, surrounded by this springlike atmosphere, had the impression that last night's snowstorm had been a mere illusion brought on by her passage through the Headless Horseman's enchanted town. Or perhaps by the sweet-smelling daiquiri that she had drunk in Sleepy Hollow. She passed two slow cars and looked at the clock. It was ten after nine. She had been at the wheel for almost eight hours. She had the sensation again that the night had been enchanted. It had passed in an instant, and she didn't feel tired at all. She was in fine form. She drove through Framingham and stopped at a gas station. There she put some coins in the telephone, dialed the number of the hotel, and asked reception to connect her with room 1311.

"They've gone out," the receptionist told her.

"Are you sure? Mr. and Mrs. Nabokov are staying in the room. I believe Mr. Nabokov hasn't gone out yet."

"Sorry, but he has gone out. I saw him."

"At what time?"

"I can't tell you. I'm not authorized to answer that kind of question."

When she reached Brighton, Véra tried again, with the same result.

She reached the hotel before ten o'clock and asked the receptionist to return the car to the rental office; she planned to get around by taxi. She went up to the thirteenth floor and headed to room 1311. She opened the door, saw that the beds were made and the room was straightened up, with Vladimir's pants and vest spread out on the chair, the nightstand, as usual, covered with books and papers. Ah! There it was! On the edge of the stand, she saw a sheet of paper that was torn from a notebook and bore Vladimir's writing:

Dearest,
If you get back early, come to the Sanders Theatre.
I have gone to rehearse the presentation for
tonight. Hurry, I can't take it any more without
you.

Your, Volodia

Véra who had planned to take a shower, decided not to. She didn't even change her clothes or have a bite of breakfast. She called reception right away to ask them to order her a taxi.

"To the Sanders Theatre! I'm in a hurry," she ordered the driver. He took off in such a rush that he sped through the crossing signs without stopping.

12

She got out of the taxi and, in her high heels, dashed straight to the door of the theater, but the door was closed. She pushed it hard but to no avail. Then she ran to the side door, with the same result.

"It's closed now, ma'am, come back at night," a well-meaning plumber told her, as he passed by with his case of tools.

"I can't wait," Véra answered, irritated. "My husband is inside."

"Ah!" the plumber exclaimed. "In that case you should tell the police."

She could not get in until an enormous cleaning woman came out.

It didn't take her long to find Vladimir in the wings, along with a number of friends from the university and two extremely good-looking girls. She found out afterward that they were two drama students the organizers had chosen to help him read during his presentation. On the table, in the middle of the cheerful group, was a bottle of red wine and a few half-full glasses. They didn't realize Véra was there since she had stayed in a dark corner. At that moment, Vladimir took a wad of ten-dollar bills out of his pocket.

"I'll give one hundred dollars to whoever guesses the name of Pushkin's father!" he said, showing off the bills with a fierce smile.

"Yes, he was called Sergey! Cheryl got it right!" his deep, baritone voice sounded over the others.

He picked up the ten-dollar bills, raised his arm, and scattered them over the girl as if they were raindrops.

The group clapped to show their appreciation. Someone photographed the scene.

At that point, Véra appeared among them and approached Vladimir.

"Volodia," she said coldly and distantly, "when you finish, come to the hotel. I'll be waiting for you in the room."

And she left, her mink coat flapping behind her.

Vladimir finished his wine, clicked his tongue, and picked up his coat. He made a face and said, "Duty calls me, my friends. We'll see each other tonight."

13

When Vladimir reached the hotel room, he felt that, instead of Véra, a big black storm cloud was waiting for him. He tried in vain to share his good mood with her. She left him on his own right away, remarking dryly that she had something to do and that she'd be back in an hour.

An hour and a quarter later, she opened the door and said, "When you have time, look over these papers."

Vladimir looked at them. He saw that Véra had canceled the cruise, planned for May 10, to celebrate in high style, with all their American friends, the forty-one years they had been together. She had also changed the reservations for their return to Europe. Now they would be leaving in three days.

14

That night, Vladimir climbed up to the illuminated set in the theater. Before he did anything else, he made sure that Véra was really seated in the center of the first row, just as the pianist Bachmann, the protagonist of one of his stories, always checked to see if his friend Madame Perov was seated in the first row of the stalls. Without her, he could not play, Véra thought and gave him a cold, satisfied smile. Filippa's pill was still having its miraculous effect. Véra felt as fresh as if she had had a good sleep the night before. She was careful, however, not to let it show. She kept herself in check.

Vladimir won the public over as soon as he opened his mouth. He was seated behind a little table with a blue-and-white teapot and a matching cup and saucer. "It must be English porcelain," Véra thought. From time to time, he took a long drink of tea and then filled the cup again. He drank it without milk and sugar and took great pleasure in it. It almost seemed as if he had come to the theater for the tea and that the gathering and the reading were secondary.

First, he told the audience what it had meant to him to translate *Eugene Onegin* into English. That translation represented twenty years of work. For months, in spurts, he had translated from nine in the morning until two at night. After a while, he realized that the translation had to be faithful. That's why he had sacrificed its rhyme and rhythm, its music and even its beauty to achieve his ideal of fidelity. The translation would be published in New York in the fall. Nabokov knew that some critics did not like that approach, including his old friend of many years, the well-known critic and writer Edmund Wilson; however, he expected comprehension and even praise from others for his heroic task.

Afterward, he told the public how he put together a novel: First he worked it all out in his head and thought it over for a good while. Then he wrote out the scenes and noted important points on index cards. His wife read them and typed them up. Over supper, Mrs. Nabokov analyzed what he had written and made suggestions about the best way to proceed. If his wife had any objections, which happened with some frequency, he rewrote the part in question. Sometimes, he spread out the typed sheets on the bed and classified them. Afterward, his wife put them away in a boot box, according to the order he had chosen. Finally, Mrs. Nabokov took them out of the box one at a time and copied them as pages.

"My wife is my first and best reader. Without her, I would never have become what I am," he proclaimed, winking at her.

She hid her reaction, delighted with that unexpected praise but careful not to let it show.

The audience rose to its feet and applauded Vladimir effusively.

After the presentation, they went to a party that their good friends Elena and Harry Levin had organized at home for the people who had attended the event. Elena toasted Véra and Vladimir on their happy marriage.

"Happy marriage? It's because I'm afraid of her and do just what she wants," Vladimir joked.

"Poor Véra," Elena defended her. "And why are you afraid of her, Volodia?"

"Will you show her why, my love?"

Without hurrying, Véra opened her beaded bag and, with a proud smile, took out a small, heavy revolver and placed it on the palm of her hand. It shone brighter than her diamond bracelet.

Someone whispered, "Is it loaded?"

Vladimir swallowed his champagne and explained slowly in a joking tone, "Of course, it's loaded—it's Véra's. In the twenties and thirties, when he lived in Berlin, a well-known Russian writer, Yuri Eichenwald, told the Germans: 'In the community of Russian emigrants, everybody knows who and what kind of person little Véra is. Little Véra is a boxer who goes into the ring and won't stop hitting her opponent until he's down.'"

Later that same night, the voluminous cleaning lady who had let Véra into the theater that morning was collecting odds and ends from the set. In the blue-and-white flowered cup the little bit of tea that was left struck her as having an odd smell. She tried it. Then she licked her lips, clicked her tongue, and finished it off. What seemed like tea tasted wonderfully like Scotch.

15

Three days later, embarking on the *Franklin D. Roosevelt*, Véra thought that if she got another letter from someone who organized literary gatherings, she would answer that Nabokov was too busy writing a new book to participate in the act to which they were inviting him. And it would be true. Vladimir would be busy writing a new book.

Vladimir gave a last look at the city that he loved best in the world. Standing on the deck, he was wearing a light-colored coat. Next to him, Véra's mink coat was shining so that it competed with the waves of the sea, which were sparkling in the warm spring sunlight. The two of them waved at Dmitri, Filippa, and the other friends and colleagues who had come to the port to say goodbye. No one laughed. It was as if they all knew that would be the last trip Vladimir and Véra made to America and that many of them would not see the couple again. Filippa looked hard at Véra's handbag, this time a bigger one than the dressy purse she took to events, and made out, once again, the shape of her little Browning. She knew then that Véra would always make sure it was loaded. Filippa would go back to Harvard that same day. Dmitri would sing two more times in *The Marriage of Figaro* before flying back to Milan.

When the ship sailed, Vladimir drew Véra's attention to a butterfly floating toward the Statue of Liberty: "Do you see it, Véra? It's a two points or common blue, a *Polyommatus icarus*. A week at sea without any butterflies is what awaits me."

IV

VLADIMIR, VÉRA, DMITRI, IRINA

Montreux, 1990

1

Like a character in a Vermeer painting, Véra was seated at an old wooden table next to the window, leaning over a book. A flat spring light filtered through the window, emphasizing her pale face and illuminating her bony hands, marked by veins like green serpents. She was eighty-eight, almost as old as the century in whose early days she was born. Once again she read a passage from *Pale Fire*, which she was translating into Russian. As she translated Vladimir's words she felt a sense of communion with her dead husband.

They had buried Vladimir in the little cemetery at Clarens in the municipality of Montreux, just below the Châtelard palace, which dominates the burial ground. Nothing in Clarens is worth remembering, except perhaps that Jean-Jacques Rousseau situated his novel *Julie, or the New Heloise* there. And Dmitri said that a music lover might remember that Tchaikovsky composed his Violin Concerto in D Major, Opus 35 there, and, forty years later, Igor Stravinsky did his own sort of thing in the same place with two well-known ballets: *The Rite of Spring* and *Pulcinella*.

After Vladimir's death, Véra was forced to leave the Palace Hotel, which closed for renovations that went on for several years. Dmitri found an apartment for her to rent halfway between the hotel and the cemetery. She led a stoic life in it, dedicated to her husband's work, which she considered a joint enterprise even though she never said that in public. She sat down next to the translations and the correspondence like a medieval monk translating classical Greek philosophy into Latin. In the letters she sent to the few friends she still had, she compared herself to Vermeer's Geographer, investigating documents piled up on the table and heaps of papers strewn over the floor.

For fifty-five years, she had taken care of the correspondence with editors and corrected the existing translations, fifty-five years reviewing and modifying new editions. And she did not dare, until after Vladimir's death, to do the translations herself; she felt now that she couldn't rely on any translator other than Dmitri or herself.

2

The night Vladimir died in the hospital in Lausanne, Dmitri put her in the blue Ferrari that he had left parked in front of the building. During the trip to Montreux, after staying quiet for a long time, Véra made a proposition: "Listen, Mitia, we'll rent a plane and crash it."

"You're not thinking seriously about that."

"We'll fly straight up, and then we'll dive to the ground."

She wanted to impress Dmitri with how seriously she was taking the death of his father: She did not want to go on living without him. But he responded with a thought he kept to himself: "You only want to make yourselves—you and Papa—famous even after his death."

3

So much time had gone by since the night when Dmitri and Filippa and she drank champagne after the performance at the Metropolitan Opera! That night Mitia was still young and full of life; his future lay before him. On the trip to America that turned out to be the last, they were all so young! It was in...yes, in 1964. Mitia was thirty-one, and Filippa eight years older. It was twenty-six years ago, and in the meantime, everything had changed.

Filippa was another one who had gone for good.

After spending those two weeks no one wished for with her in Nice, Vladimir and Véra ran into her again in 1964 at Harvard, and Véra went with her to the opera in New York. After the night at the opera and Vladimir's presentation at the theater in Harvard, they had returned straightaway to Europe. Véra had organized it that way. Their brief stay in the United States turned out to be their last one. Not just because Vladimir had begun to suffer all sorts of problems with his health but also because—if she were to be totally fair—Véra refused to visit again. Vladimir felt so drawn to the country she had the feeling, when he was there, that she had lost control of him.

They kept a correspondence going with Filippa or, to be more precise, Véra responded from time to time to the avalanche of letters Filippa sent their way. She didn't write the sort of letters of which Véra approved; they weren't sensible letters in which she expressed her gratitude for their help in getting her installed in America or explained that she was following their wise advice and, as a result, was leading an emotionally stable life. Far from it! Instead of a rational narrative, she sent them her impressions several times a week. She was constantly asking, "When, in God's name, are you going to take off that mask, Véra? When are you going to show me who you really are?" She repeated and repeated variations on this theme. Véra didn't realize that it was Filippa's psychological distress that spoke, so— not understanding her extravagant behavior—she asked Filippa to put an end to her stream of letters. She wrote it coldly and dryly...and rationally.

Some things were clear from the verbal sediment and the pathos that characterized Filippa's letters. Filippa felt that having been uprooted from her native Sweden, she had betrayed herself. She could no longer see her life clearly. She had gotten lost in the unlimited possibilities that America—and, in fact, the whole world—offered once she left home. Indirectly, she blamed Véra and, more than once, accused her of trying to live her own life through her young friend, saying that Véra's dream had been not only to write but also to publish books that were a critical and commercial success and so to become in her own right a famous writer with an international reputation. Her lack of talent had made that impossible, and once she had acknowledged it, she had tried to project her own ambition onto other people: first onto the life and art of Vladimir and now onto Filippa's life and—not yet realized—art. She had insisted that Filippa, a poet, write only novels, and, as she had done with Vladimir, she pressured her to abandon her Swedish, like a dirty dishrag, and write in English and also to change countries and milieus. She even tried to monitor Filippa's personal life, her relationship with her girlfriend. She accused her repeatedly of being "imprudent and crazy" for living with a woman. Véra organized the lives of the people around her who were not strong enough to resist her constant pressure. As a result, they sacrificed their own ideals, they became strangers to themselves and no longer knew what they wanted out of life. Véra read the Swede's reproaches over and over with some care. Finally, however, she had had enough of the woman she called "irrational Filippa" and asked her lawyers to help her end that exhausting series of letters.

Filippa spent a month in a psychiatric clinic; there they stuffed her with tranquilizers that turned out to be useless in the long run. She stayed on in the United States, where she never really fit in, and tried to commit suicide more than once. She died a year after Vladimir, in September 1978, from an advanced case of kidney cancer. Véra was happy to have rid herself of that uncomfortable correspondence thanks to the lawyers and had not given Filippa a moment's thought up until her death.

4

Véra looked out through the window and distinguished in the spring garden a black cat that ran toward the house, crossed the little path, and then lay down in wait. Dmitri used to laugh at his mother, since it wasn't a black cat but the barbecue that was one of the odd bits in the garden. But for Véra, it was a black cat.

Another matter was pending, and it lay in wait just like the cat in the garden. She still had not burned the unfinished manuscript of *The Original of Laura*. When Vladimir began to realize that he was dying, he had asked her to burn it, again and again! It was his last wish. Véra, however, decided not to tell anyone and to finish it herself in such a way that no one would be aware of the switch. She knew Vladimir's baroque style as if it were her own, with the narrative slowly unwinding in the odd English he had used in the last decades. She had typed out most of his novels more than once. In her judgment, the unfinished novel opened a new direction in Vladimir's work, a direction in which there was less description and more direct action. She knew what was missing in the novel: Many passages were just sketched out; the text needed color and flavor; at many points, it needed a bridge between description and dialogue. She tried to do it and, after reading what she had done, realized she wasn't up to it. Her result was an insipid Nabokov, like a weak child just recovering from a serious illness. She tried again and again with her door locked tight. She had not even told Mitia. But every one of her attempts was a failure. She realized how wise she had been to measure her strengths and relinquish any idea of a career in the arts.

For the time being, she put away Vladimir's unfinished manuscript in the safe-deposit box at the bank. Only Mitia knew it existed. Véra was careful not to mention it ever to anyone, but she must have let it slip with Dmitri, because not long ago Knopf, the American publishing house, had written to let her know that the editor in chief would like to have a look at the manuscript and would travel to Montreux to do so. Véra knew that it wasn't what Vladimir wanted, but she didn't have the strength to go to the bank, open the safe-deposit box, take out the hundred and thirty-eight index cards of the manuscript, and either show them to the editor or, better yet, burn them all. She knew she should do it, but she could not. She didn't have it in her. After her death, Dmitri could decide what to do. Lately, it was hard for her to make any decisions. They wore her out. To tell the truth, Vladimir's manuscript meant so much to her that she didn't want to decide its fate, and further-more...yes, this was the truth: She would never, ever be able to burn the much loved manuscript.

Véra finished her answer to the editor in chief of Knopf and opened the journal in which, after Vladimir's death, she had begun to note down scenes from her husband's life in an effort to understand him. But she was still left with the old feeling—deep-rooted and familiar from all the years of her marriage—that there was no way to really understand him. Nevertheless, she kept on trying.

Once again, she felt like the figure in her favorite Ver-meer, *The Lacemaker*, absorbed in her work, illuminated by the light of the window, almost blessed by that light as if she were a modern saint dedicated to an arduous task. The same look with which Véra used to see her husband when he was alive was now directed at his photograph, positioned on top of the desk.

Dmitri was entering his mother's office just at that moment. Seeing her in profile, he confirmed for the hundredth time that her expression revealed loyalty, ardor, and even exaltation. He turned away so as not to disturb her.

5

Véra had also looked for traces of Irina. She knew intuitively that *Lolita* reflected the pain he felt on losing the woman he had loved in Paris, especially in the second part of the novel, where readers are no longer angry at Humbert Humbert because they feel compassion for him in his misery. She was the only one who realized that in this part Nabokov was speaking of his own agony.

After Vladimir's death, she calmed down and stopped thinking about Irina as an evil nymph. She found out that, after the young woman's brief and intense relationship with Vladimir, she had not had any other lovers, nor found a husband or regular companion. Irina Guadanini kept on living primarily through her memories and writing poems, most of them directed at Vladimir. After the Second World War, she moved from Paris to Munich, where she worked in the editing office of Radio Free Europe. In 1962, she published, at her own expense, a book of her poems written under the influence of Anna Akhmatova in a run of three hundred copies, under the title *Letters*. Carrying a little package that contained a few copies of the newly edited book in her suitcase, she traveled to the United States, where she tried to find Vladimir, but none of her emigrant friends could help her. At that time, Nabokov had already published *Lolita* and had become a famous American writer; later he would be proposed repeatedly for the Nobel Prize. In hopes that her poems would reach his hands, Irina sent copies of her book to a number of American libraries. Among the poems, there is one entitled "Cremona" and dedicated to Giovanni Battista Guadanini, the grandfather from Cremona. A few poems speak of excursions to the countryside, but the majority of them dwell on what she had experienced and lost: the poems "Geminis," "Happiness," "Date," and "Gift," among others. In "The Tunnel," a narrative that makes up the last part of *Letters*, she confesses in a highly stylized form her feelings for Vladimir. It ends with an imaginary suicide. Some of the poems hint that Irina believed Vladimir wrote her letters. She relates many passages in his novels to his relationship with her.

And she was right. Véra knew that Vladimir had been inspired by the experience of being torn between the two women when he wrote *The Real Life of Sebastian Knight*, a novel describing the hell brought on by a love triangle. She saw from the first few pages that when he described the horrors of life with his lover, he was trying to convince himself that the decision to stay with his family was right. He was trying to persuade himself even though he didn't believe it or, to be precise, *because* he didn't believe it.

Twenty years later, he found inspiration in Irina once again when he wrote *Pnin*. The book begins with the protagonist, a Russian emigrant who lives in the United States, setting off by train to give a talk in Cremona although there is no city in the United States with that name. Cremona was clearly a reference to Irina. It was the story of Vladimir's reading tour through the States. One of the cities he visited was Florence in South Carolina. Irina is embodied in the character Liza Bogolepov. She has Irina's eyes. Véra remembered them clearly: On the beach at Cannes, Irina's eyes were bluer than the sea in the spring sun. There's more: Liza and Pnin meet each other just as Irina and Nabokov did, that is, after his talk. Like Irina, Liza is also a poet even though Vladimir spoke critically of her poems, which pleased Véra no end. Liza is shown (probably unlike Irina, thought Véra, proud of her effort at fairness) as being motivated by her own interests. Nevertheless, Timofey Pnin, the author's alter ego—it is the most autobiographical of Nabokov's novels—declares he had always loved Liza and that his feelings would never change. In that way, Vladimir was clearly paying homage to the woman he loved long ago.

Véra also found a brief note that Vladimir wrote in his diary on the same day Irina died although he was unaware of her death. The note said he felt out of sorts all that day without knowing why. Not only had he never forgotten her, Véra thought, but he was somehow psychically in communication with her in spite of the distance and the many years that separated them. Even in death.

6

She tried to concentrate on the translation, but that morning her thoughts flew in every direction, like butterflies hovering over a meadow in the spring. She got up and went out into the hall. Those photos... Dmitri and his trophies... Why did Dmitri want to display those disturbing photos of his accidents all over the apartment?

Even that last one, three years after Vladimir's death. Véra tried to ward off the thought about what happened that day, but it wasn't easy for her. The images came to mind so vividly. On September 26, 1980, Dmitri was driving his Ferrari 308 GTB, a car meant for racing, at top speed from Lausanne to Montreux so he wouldn't be late for lunch with his mother. At that speed, the car missed a tight turn on the highway, spun out of its lane, and caught on fire. Thanks to a miracle, or perhaps his own agility, Dmitri managed to get out of the car with his hair, his hands, and his torso in flames. From the hospital where they took him with serious burns and broken vertebrae, he called his mother to say he wouldn't be able to make lunch because he had had a little accident. Once he had hung up, he lost consciousness.

Véra spent ten months visiting her son from the other side of the window of the intensive care unit. He had suffered third-degree burns on forty percent of his body. She watched him for ten months, lying in bed with his face and body bandaged. Against all common sense, she imagined that when they took off his bandages and the cast, he would jump out of bed and everything would go back to normal.

Those ten months of daily visits were relatively happy compared to what came after.

One day, in his hospital room, he appeared in a wheelchair and, for the first time, with no bandages on his face. He had lowered the light on purpose. Véra saw what she would have preferred never ever to see, something that looked more like the monster out of a horror film than a man. She was hoping it was just a nightmare. When she looked at that strange form in the wheelchair, she could not overcome her panic, a mixture of repugnance and the deepest compassion, a panic so intense that it paralyzed her.

Little by little, she got used to the idea that this deformed, immobile, aged figure was her child and that the playful, youthful Mitia, her little goat, would never come back. When she was not with him, helping with his physical therapy and the practical considerations of his new life, she rushed home to bury herself in the mounting correspondence about the new editions and the translations of Vladimir's books. The heap of work distracted her from the thoughts that her passion for luxury sports cars and love of speed had been transmitted to her beloved son, the only person left to her. Those thoughts pursued her like the heartless goddesses who took revenge on Orestes.

The car crash put an end to Dmitri's successful career as an opera singer. He lost his flexibility and mobility, and even after a long rehabilitation he could only walk slowly and with a cane. Under his mother's direction, he began, like her, to dedicate himself totally to his father's work, although it had been exactly what he had sought to avoid in order to live his own life, out of the shadow of his famous progenitor. Secretly, Véra felt the satisfaction of having led Dmitri to where she always wanted him to go.

At that time, many people expressed their sympathy for her, but she would have none of it. She did not want to share with anyone what she was going through. She sealed herself in behind a black mask of inaccessibility. She always held her head high. When she spoke with people, she was even colder and more austere than she had been. Only occasionally did she see, in someone's look, a spark of understanding, a realization that her reserve was the effort of a fragile and vulnerable woman to hide something she had never experienced before.

7

Véra went back to her desk. She had had a good look at the shadow that some time ago had fumbled its way into the office where she worked on the translations. It was the shadow of an overweight, rigid man, a kind of golem with a cane. She felt relief when the shadow withdrew as silently as it had entered.

Another time, she looked at the cat in the garden. A black cat, like her Browning, kept as always in the bottom of the first drawer of the desk inside the beaded evening purse. Véra opened the drawer, put her hand on the velvet purse, and felt it to make sure that the revolver was still there. She knew it was loaded. She always took it with her when she went out in the evening, just as she had done with

Vladimir. She had never used it, but being aware that it was near helped her to live, like tranquilizers do for some people. The loaded revolver in her purse.

She looked at the cat and then thought that in the end she had led the two men in her life, her husband and her son, where she wanted them to go. She had had Vladimir in her hands from the moment they settled down in Montreux. Dmitri also depended on her now, although at a price that was much too high.

8

Véra put the notebook aside and directed her gaze to the clouds that were moving slowly in the sky. From the west to the east, from Geneva toward Valais, she thought with her characteristic precision.

She felt as though she were navigating in a soft white cloud through a blue sky and that she observed everything from on high, as if she were above earthly concerns. "But they are the dead, not I!" The thought surprised her at the same time that she shook her head. Nevertheless, an intense pain in her vertebrae seized her, and she preferred to turn her attention to the book of Vladimir's that she was translating.

BIBLIOGRAPHY

Berberova, Nina. *The Italics Are Mine*. NY: Alfred Knopf, 1992.

———. *Nabokov i ego Lolita* (Nabokov and his Lolita). Moscow: Izdatelstvo (Publishers) Sabashnikovykh, 1998.

Boyd, Brian. *Vladimir Nabokov: The American Years*. Princeton, NJ: Princeton University Press, 1991.

———. *Vladimir Nabokov: The Russian Years*. Princeton, NJ: Princeton University Press, 1990.

Guadanini, Irina, *Pisma* (Letters). St. Petersburg, Russia: Renome, 2012.

Karlinsky, Simon, editor. *The Nabokov–Wilson Letters 1940–1971*. London: Weidenfeld and Nicolson, 1979.

Nabokov, Vladimir. *Letters to Véra*. Edited by Olga Voronina and Brian Boyd. NY: Vintage International, 2017.

———. *Nabokov's Quartet*. NY: Phaedra, 1966.

———. *Novels and Memoirs 1941–1951*. NY: Library of America, 1987.

———. *Novels 1955–1962*. NY: Library of America, 1988.

———. *Novels 1969–1974*. NY: Library of America, 1989.

———. *Poems*. London: Weidenfeld and Nicolson, 1961.

———. *Poems and Problems*. London: Weidenfeld and Nicolson, 1972.

———. *Polnoe sobranie stikhotvorenii* (Complete poetry). RoyalLib.com.

———. *Selected Poems*. Edited by Thomas Karshan, translated by Dmitri Nabokov. NY: Knopf, 2012.

———. *Sobranie sochinenii amerikanskogo perioda* (Complete works from the American period). St. Petersburg: Symposium Publishing House, 2000.

———. *Sobranie sochinenii russkogo perioda* (Complete works from the Russian period). St. Petersburg: Symposium Publishing House, 2000.

Roper, Robert. *Nabokov in America*. NY: Bloomsbury, 2015.

Schiff, Stacy. *Véra (Mrs. Vladimir Nabokov)*. NY: Random House, 1999.

Weinman, Sarah. *The Real Lolita: The Kidnapping of Sally Horner and the Novel that Scandalized the World*. NY: Harper Collins, 2018.

MONIKA ZGUSTOVA is an award-winning author whose works have been published in ten languages. She was born in Prague and studied comparative literature in the United States (University of Illinois and University of Chicago). She then moved to Barcelona, where she writes for *El País, The Nation,* and *CounterPunch,* among others. As a translator of Czech and Russian literature into Spanish and Catalan—including the writing of Havel, Kundera, Hrabal, Hašek, Dostoyevsky, Akhmatova, Tsvetaeva, and Babel—Zgustova is credited with bringing major twentieth-century writers to Spain. Her book *Dressed for a Dance in the Snow: Women's Voices from the Gulag* was published by Other Press in 2020.

JULIE JONES is Professor Emeritus of Spanish at the University of New Orleans. She has published widely on the Latin American writers of the "Boom," with a focus on Luis Buñuel's work, in numerous articles for journals such as *Cineaste* and *Cinema Journal.*